the MOST IMPORTANT THING

the MOST IMPORTANT THING

STORIES ABOUT SONS, FATHERS AND GRANDFATHERS

by AVI

WALKER BOOKS
AND SUBSIDIARIES

LONDON • BOSTON • SYDNEY • AUCKLAND

For David Miller

This edition first published 2017 in Australia by
Walker Books Australia Pty Ltd, Locked Bag 22, Newtown
NSW 2042 Australia and in Great Britain by
Walker Books Ltd, 87 Vauxhall Walk, London SE11 5HJ

"Kitchen Table" is a revised version of a story published in the
anthology *The Color of Absence* (Simon and Schuster, 2001).

"Beat Up" appeared in another form in the anthology
From One Experience to Another (Forge, 1997).

Typeset in ITC Mendoza

Printed and bound in Great Britain by Clays Ltd, St Ives plc

A Cataloguing-in-Publication entry is available from the
National Library of Australia catalogue: http://catalogue.nla.gov.au/

British Library Cataloguing in Pubication Data: a catalogue
record for this book is available from the British Library

ISBN 978-1-925381-63-4

www.walkerbooks.com.au
www.walker.co.uk

"What's the most important thing you can do for your son?"

Contents

DREAM CATCHER

My dad woke me at six, and by six thirty, he was gripping the leather-covered wheel of his black BMW, with me barely awake, sitting shotgun. He drove as fast as a getaway car trying to get away from something. I had no idea what. But then, our conversations consisted mostly of slapping silences at each other, like phantom Ping-Pong players.

Which was why, though he was my father, I knew as much about him as I did about one of those lions sitting outside the city's main library. He was there and in charge, but when he talked, it was mostly about rules and expectations, as predictable as a self-winding watch, with smiles as rare as snowballs in August. I could sum up his view on life in five words: *Be ready for the worst.*

Anyway, by seven thirty, we were sitting at Gate 44 at LaGuardia Airport in NYC, with pale lemon sunlight seeping through the plate-glass windows. Most travelers were slumped in hard leather chairs, eyes lidded, occasionally checking cell phones, probably wishing someone cared about their leaving. A few others, bags at their feet, stood by the closed gate door as if nervous that they might be left behind. Overhead television monitors showed the world's latest disasters in gory color. No one seemed to care.

I had my eyes on a brown sparrow, which had gotten inside the terminal. He kept banging against the big windows, trying to fly free. He couldn't. The whole airport was for flying, and here was the one creature that *could* fly, and he was trapped. Then again, by flying, I was trapped. I think my eighth-grade English teacher would have called this *irony*.

So there I was, new travel bag at my feet, stiff new jeans, a collared shirt, a new jacket, and a haircut that was too short. All this so I would look the way my father wanted me to look.

My father, the chief financial officer for a window-making company, was in his work uniform: dark suit, pale-blue shirt, striped blue tie with a Windsor knot, and a matching pale-blue handkerchief poking out of his jacket breast pocket like a mouse too timid to come out of his hole. Dad's trimmed hair, flecked with gray, was combed back with care. The creases in his trousers were snap-sharp, his face was baby-belly smooth, and he smelled of cologne—his way, I think, of informing people he was alive.

After sitting silently for ten minutes, he said, "I expect your visit to your grandfather will go well."

"What makes you expect that?"

"Paul," he said, "if I have learned anything, it's that people get on better when they do what they have to do. There's an old saying," he went on. "'Learn the rules. Play the rules. Win and you get to change the rules.' I should also say, If rules are not followed, things fall apart.

"That's why," he added as he always did, "you need to be ready for the worst."

I said, "Guess what? I'd rather not play."

When he made no reply, I said, "When was the last time you spoke to your father?"

"Two days ago, when I set this up."

"No, before. Like, what, two, three years ago? You guys aren't exactly chatty, are you? And I've never met him, right? Most of all, you don't like him. How come?"

He just sat there.

I said, "I know nothing about him. Oh, yeah — he lives in Denver. But we don't have any pictures of him, so I don't even know what he looks like. He's a complete stranger, but I'm visiting him. If you don't like him, why should I?"

My dad did his library lion likeness, and then said, "I'll go over it again. There's a big company audit this week, and I'm in charge. Endless hours. Late hours. By bad luck, your mother is having unexpected surgery, which, while not a big thing, means she'll need to take it easy and will stay with your aunt. As it happens, you have spring break. I don't want you to be home alone."

Knowing where he was going, it was my turn to say nothing.

So he said, "Three weeks ago, when your mother and I were late getting back because of a canceled flight, meaning you were alone on Saturday night, what happened?"

I said, "I had a few friends over."

"Fifteen friends are not a few. Paul, when you can't trust your family, you wind up not trusting anyone.

"We couldn't call your mom's parents," he went on. "They're away. We called some of your friends' parents. They couldn't help. Too short a notice. But my father was willing for you to come and stay with him."

I said, "In other words, there was no one else to babysit me, so you called your father. Bottom of the barrel, totally. We see Mom's dad and mom every other weekend. You call him Dad; her, Mom. I've never even heard you mention *your* mother. We *never* see or talk to *your* father. Now, all of sudden I'm flying across the country to spend a week with him. I'm closer to the moon than to him."

No response.

I said, "What is it? Did he have bad breath, wear socks that didn't match, make you eat gluten-free food? I just want to know why you dislike him so much."

"Maybe it's time you found out."

"Find out *what?*"

"When you get off the plane," he said, "your grandfather promised he'll be waiting. Soon as you meet him, use your cell phone to call your mom. She'll be wanting to hear from you. Otherwise, she'll worry."

"What if he breaks his promise and he's *not* there?"

He actually took my question seriously. "Call my secretary."

"If you'd just tell me *why* you don't like your dad, you could save the price of a ticket to Denver."

"You'll be back next Sunday."

A new thought popped into my head. "Wait a minute!" I said. "Is it that he doesn't like *you?*"

"I'll give you a tip: keep your smart mouth shut."

A loudspeaker voice said, "Attention please! We are ready to start boarding Flight 633 with service to Denver."

Dad led me to the check-in counter, where he laid down my ticket and some papers. "I'm Michael Gunderson," he announced. "This is my son. Paul Gunderson. Unaccompanied minor." He showed his driver's license. "His grandfather will be at the Denver gate. If the boy gives you any difficulties, let me know. My number is on the papers."

He didn't even say *my* boy—just *the* boy.

The woman smiled at me. "I'm sure he'll be fine."

I gave my father a snappy military salute, but it was wasted on him because he was already moving away, keeping to his schedule and, I'm sure, ready for the worst.

A gatekeeper led me onto the plane. None of the seats were occupied. "You're 24F—window seat," the guy said, and shoved my bag into the bin over my head. "Enjoy your flight."

I buckled up and watched the ground crew fling suitcases around as if they were garbage bags. I was thinking, *My father doesn't like his father, but he won't say why. Or maybe his father doesn't like him. So keep your mouth shut and be ready for the worst. You're about to spend a week with a stranger.*

My plane touched down at Denver International Airport something like four and a half hours later. Because I was required to stay with a flight attendant, I was one of the last people to get off. When we reached the end of the exit lane, I studied the people standing, in search of someone who looked like my dad.

"Do you see your grandfather?" asked the attendant.

"Don't know what he looks like."

Even as I spoke, a man came forward. He was tall and skinny with a pale, gaunt face. The shadowy bags under his eyes were big enough to pack for a month's vacation. He was wearing khaki trousers, khaki shirt, and a blue cap, which proclaimed *Viet Vet* in embroidered gold. The resemblance to my father was creepy: it was as if my father had become an old guy.

"Paul?" he said to me. It came as a question, as if he couldn't — or wouldn't — believe it was me. "Paul Gunderson?"

I held up my hand, like a kid asking a teacher if I could leave the room. Which, right then, I would have liked to do, though the room was a gigantic airport terminal.

The flight attendant asked, "Are you Mr. Gunderson?"

"It's what people call me," the guy said. He seemed reluctant to admit it.

While papers were exchanged, and a driver's license checked, I stared at my grandfather — for that's who I assumed he was — trying to make some sense of him. Right off, he didn't seem friendly. Not a trace of a smile.

Next moment, I realized the flight attendant had abandoned me. That left my grandfather and me to confront each other like two aliens meeting in space; the only thing in common was that we lived in the same universe.

"Hello," he said, as if it were the last thing he wanted to say. He even hesitated before holding out a hand. It was obvious: he was as reluctant to meet me as I was to meet him.

All the same, we shook, his hand being hard and stiff.

"Need to stop for food?" he asked. "It's twenty minutes to my truck. Thirty minutes to my home."

"I probably won't starve."

He gave me a quizzical look, as if not sure if I was trying to be funny. I pretended not to notice.

"Check any bags?"

"Nope."

"Good," he said, and led the way along what felt like an endless concourse. Our silence felt equally endless. Now and again, he stole a glance at me, as if trying to decide who I was. I was trying to decide if I should tell him I really was his grandson.

After a while, he said, "You like to be called Paul? Pauly? Something else?"

"Paul works."

"Fine. Paul. People call me Road. Real name Joad, but your father, when he started talking, called me Road. It stuck. How old are you?"

"Thirteen."

"You look a lot like your father when he was that age."

"That good or bad?"

He stared straight ahead. "Not sure."

We continued on without talking until he said, "Your mother okay?"

"I was supposed to call her when I arrived."

"Then do it." The tone and command were the way my father talked, an order.

I put down my bags, took out my cell phone. A message popped up telling me the battery was very low. I called quickly. "Hi, Mom. It's me. In Denver. He's right here. Did you want to talk to him? Okay, I will. Bye."

I looked at Road. "She said to say hello, so, hello."

"You're a comedian."

I said, "If people laugh."

"I don't," he said, as if I hadn't noticed.

We started walking again. After five minutes, he said, "I never met your mother. Mickey didn't—doesn't—want me to."

It took me a moment to get that "Mickey" was my father. Back home he was always called Michael.

Road said, "You have brothers or sisters?"

I shook my head, realizing only then that he really knew as little about me as I did about him.

We went on, not talking. His conversational skills made my father seem like one of those shouting sports announcers on ESPN.

In the parking section, he led me to an old Ford pickup truck. "Looks old but it runs new," he said. "Like me. Throw your stuff in the back."

As I dropped my bags in, I noticed the license plate: A red fringe of mountains was depicted along the top. To one side of the number, there was a picture of people in a wagon. Under the number was the word *pioneer*.

"What's *pioneer* mean?" I asked.

"I get that because my ancestor came out

here before 1876, when Colorado became a state. He was looking for gold."

"Did he find any?"

"Fool's gold."

"What's that?"

"Nothing but glitter. All labor. No loot."

I hauled myself into the truck cab on a seat that had a rip. Dangling from the rearview mirror post was what looked like a spiderweb made of red string, held together by a circle of twigs.

"What's that?" I asked.

"Dream catcher," said Road, putting on sunglasses. "Ojibwe Indian culture. They say it will catch dreams. You dream much?" he asked.

"Not really. You?"

"Yeah. Lots. Nightmares. Seat belts are the law out here."

"What kind of nightmares?" I asked.

"The kind that happen if you don't wear a seat belt."

I buckled up.

As we drove out of the airport and onto the highway, Road pointed toward the west. "That's Denver," he said.

The distant tall buildings looked like a row of stubby birthday candles that had fizzled out. Beyond them were high mountains. It was late April but the summits were still snowcapped. "Does that snow stay all year?" I asked.

"Some of it never melts."

Wondering if he ever melted, I studied the sky, endless blue without a cloud. I said, "How come my father doesn't want my mother to meet you?"

"Probably thought I'd scare her away."

"Would you?"

Road kept his eyes on the highway. Then he said, "You're not here long enough to hear the all of it."

I was thinking, *It's already too long.*

We drove on. Road said, "You worried about your mother?"

"My dad says I shouldn't."

He said, "You always do what your dad says?"

"He's the boss."

"Really?"

"He thinks so."

Road said, "How is he?"

"Okay, I guess."

"Just guess?"

I said, "He makes windows, but he's not exactly transparent."

"That sounds like an old joke."

"It is."

Road didn't crack a smile, and it took a few more moments before he said, "Your dad and I don't get along."

"How come?"

He thought some more and then said, "My son—your dad—lives like the guy who drives by mostly checking the rearview mirror. See who might be catching up."

"Who's catching up?" I asked.

"Me," he said. It was a small word, but he managed to stuff a whole lot of anger into it. Eyeing him, I decided that he—thin, wiry, and with a bite—was like a snake ready to strike. I leaned away.

"Anyway," he went on, "as things now stand, you might say you're my only living relative."

"What about my dad?"

Road grunted. "I said *living*." After a moment, he added, "I say what I think."

I said, "What about thinking about what you're saying?"

"You've got a smart mouth."

"Beats a dumb one," I said, edging even farther away.

When I saw the muscle lines of his jaw clench, I remembered my father's suggestion: to keep my mouth shut. As it was, Road was silent for quite a while until he said, "What kind of things you like to do?"

"Hanging out with friends. TV. Video games. Music."

"Guess what? I hate cell phones, and I have no TV. Despise it. Nothing but bad news and ads, telling you what to do. What about sports?"

"I like football."

"If you want to hurt people, join the army."

We drove on. I said, "Do you work?"

He snorted. "Live on my Social Security. Veteran's pension. Used to be a carpenter. Catch an odd job now and then in the neighborhood. I have one this week. Nothing big. Enough to buy you some food."

Deciding I seriously didn't like him, I put my eyes on the mountains to the west. They looked like gigantic jagged walls, and I was trapped behind them for a week.

Half an hour later, he said, "Here we are."

Ogden Street was lined with trees, a fair number of daffodils, and brick houses. Road's house was the smallest — a one-story brick, with a steeply pitched roof and a tall chimney. Looked like a goblin's house.

"Built in the 1920s," he said. "Back when there was a trolley line on this street."

"What's a trolley?"

"Huh! Visiting me must be like time travel for you. Trolley is a street railway."

We walked into the front room, which took up most of the house. One wall was entirely covered with bookcases, stuffed with books. I had never seen so many in a house. A big easy chair. A reading lamp. A fireplace. No logs. Two windows. Over both windows hung more dream catchers. No pictures on the walls. At the far end of the main room was a small kitchen with a counter and stools. Landline phone on the wall.

There was a side hall, with a small room that led off from it; a bathroom; and up front, a bedroom. On the ceiling of the hallway a recessed square. Hanging down from it was a loop of rope that looked like a noose.

"What's that for?" I asked, pointing up.

"Pulls down a folding staircase which leads to a storage attic. Full of junk. This is your room," said Road, indicating the extra room in the back.

It was a small room with pale-green walls. One window—with another dream catcher—a narrow bed, a dresser, and a chair. Another wall of books. I might as well have checked in to a library.

"Was this my dad's room?"

"It was meant to be, but he took off when I got this place."

"Took off?"

"Left. Never came back. You a reader?"

"Not really."

"Your loss. Put your things a\
make lunch." He walked off.

Knowing I had to juice up my cell p\
I looked for my charger plug. I couldn't f\
it, which meant I had left it at home. In other
words, I was cut off from all my friends and
games.

I sat on the bed and stared at the books.
They were mostly histories of the West, cow-
boys, gold mines, and ranching. I had no idea
how I would live through the next seven days. I
thought about the noose hanging from the ceiling. Maybe I'd need it.

Road called, "Eats!"

We sat on the stools at the kitchen counter.
He still had his Viet cap on. There was a pathetic
ham-and-cheese sandwich with white bread on
a plate for me. Nothing for him.

"What do you drink? Milk? Coke? Water?"

"Coke."

"I'll get some."

As I ate, he sat opposite, not talking. He was
staring at me.

"You look just like Mickey," he told me for

the second time. Then he said, "Sounds like you two don't get along."

"It's okay."

Head bent, he studied his hands. With his cap down, I couldn't see his face. Without looking up, he said, "Does he ever talk about me?"

"No."

He looked up. "His mother?"

I shook my head.

I thought he might say more, but he didn't. Instead, he sat there until abruptly, he jumped off his seat, walked toward the front door, wheeled around, yanked off his cap, and in an angry voice, cried out, "I don't hear from Mickey for years. Then, out of the blue, he calls and tells me his wife is in the hospital and his kid — you — is coming. What kind of crap is that?"

Stunned by his anger, I said, "Do — do you want me to leave?"

"Your ticket is for next Sunday."

"I — I could change it."

"Trust me, I checked. It costs too much. I don't have the money. You're here until Sunday. I have a patio. I'll be out there."

As if trying to escape, he shot by. Momentarily, a back door banged.

Dazed, I remained at the kitchen counter, my appetite lost, not sure what to do. All I could think was: *He's crazy. I have to get out of here.* I went to my room, got out my cell phone, only to remember it was dead. There was that phone in the kitchen, but I was afraid he might come back and listen. I didn't use it.

Sitting there, I thought, *No wonder my father doesn't like this guy.* For the first time in my life, I felt sympathy for my dad. *Is that why he sent me here? To see what a jerk his father was?*

I don't know how long it took me to get up my nerve to edge out the back door. Road was sitting on a faded and torn couch, apparently just staring at the small grass yard, in the middle of which stood a concrete birdbath. No water in it. No birds.

I stood there for a while, but Road didn't seem to notice me. I said, "I want to go home."

"You can't," he said. "Suck it up." Then he said, "I get angry." It was a statement, not an apology. "Just leave me alone. I do stupid things."

That sounded like a threat.

I retreated into the house, trying to decide what to do. I didn't see how I could get home. Deciding it would be best to keep out of his way, I started for my room, but curious, I snuck into his room.

His bedroom had a narrow bed, a small table next to it, and a bureau. Nothing else. There was one window, with another dream catcher hanging from the frame. All I could think was, *He really must have lots of nightmares.*

I was about to leave the room when I noticed a small framed picture on one wall, the only picture on the walls in the whole house. It was a black and white photo of a kid, someone about my age. When I looked at it, it took me a while to realize it was my dad.

Next to Road's bed was a small table with a drawer. Listening to make sure he hadn't come back into the house, I slid it open. A pistol lay there.

Really scared, I sat in my room trying to decide what to do. The image of that pistol and Road's words—*I do stupid things*—wouldn't

leave my head. I considered finding a police station. *Get out of here,* I kept thinking.

When Road didn't appear, I went out back.
He hadn't moved.

"Going for a walk," I said.

"I'm not going anywhere," he said, sweet as
a rusty nail.

I stepped out onto the sidewalk but had no
idea where to go. I started walking. At the corner, I looked down the street. In the distance, I
could see the mountains. I walked toward them.
Not because I thought I'd get there, but because
I needed a direction.

Seven blocks later, I reached a big park.
There were joggers, people playing volleyball,
and others doing exercises, as well as kids shooting baskets. I went over to the court and stood
there, watching. After a while one of the kids
shot me a bounce pass. I took it as an invitation,
and played.

An hour later, the kids took off. I had half
a mind to ask if I could go with them. I didn't.
Not knowing what else to do, I headed back
down the same street I'd come — mountains at

my back—until I found Road's house. I stood outside for a while, until, reluctantly, I walked in. He was sitting in his large chair, reading a book. His cap was still on. It was as if he was branded with the words *Viet Vet*.

He looked up with those tired eyes of his and for a moment, just stared at me. I could almost see what he was thinking, that I looked like my father. Maybe that was his problem. All he said, however, was, "Where were you?"

"At the park, playing basketball with some kids."

"Good," he said, and went back to his reading.

He made a dinner: some packaged frozen meat loaf, with potatoes and peas. He had gotten some Coke. Doughnuts for dessert.

We didn't really talk. The click of forks and knives on plates, and sounds of chewing, seemed loud. He asked me what grade I was in, and what were my favorite subjects; the questions adults ask kids when they can't think of anything to say. He knew kids like cats know computers.

"The food okay?" he asked.

"Yeah."

"What do you eat for breakfast?"

"Oatmeal."

"You have a lot of friends?"

"Sure."

But no questions about my father—his son—or my mother. No mention of his outburst. Didn't really ask anything about me. And I was afraid to ask him about that pistol.

All the same, I'd catch him staring at me, as if he were trying to make sense of me. Or was he looking at Mickey? When I returned his gaze, he'd avert his eyes.

Dinner done, he said, "Get yourself a book. That's the entertainment here. Tomorrow, we're going up into the mountains. Camp out."

"I'm—I'm not sure I want to."

"You don't have a choice," he said.

Upset, I went to my room. *Why are we going camping? What's going to happen? Should I run away? How am I going to get out of this?*

I found a book called *The Outlaw Trail: Butch Cassidy and His Wild Bunch,* which I tried to read but couldn't—too much killing. Instead,

I lay in bed trying to make sense of Road. The best I could come up with was that he was a time bomb, like those suicide bombers you see in the news.

Wondering how and when he would explode, I fell into fitful sleep.

By eight o'clock the next morning, we were in Road's truck, moving fast, with two duffel bags in the back. Road gripped the steering wheel like my father did, tightly with two hands, his eyes locked on the road. He had his cap on, like it was a crown.

I was strapped in a seat belt, feeling as if I were being kidnapped. The dream catcher hanging from the rearview mirror post swung back and forth like a pendulum in an old clock. Or a time bomb. Though I wished I knew where we were going and why, I didn't say anything, but wondered if Road could hear my heart pounding.

We got on a freeway, drove through suburbs, then swung west on three-lane Interstate 70. As the highway slanted sharply up, snowcapped mountains loomed before us. In moments, we were among them, as if being swallowed.

After twenty minutes of silent driving, Road said, "Denver is another word for dull. But the mountains, they're something special."

Still going higher, we sped by some small towns, but didn't stop. A few times Road pointed and said, "That's a played-out mine. Probably a hundred years old. Or older. They dug deep, took what they could, and left. Colorado history is boom and bust. Mostly bust. Like me."

For the most part, all I could see were tall green trees, and mountains capped with snow. Here and there were cascading waterfalls. "Spring snowmelt," said Road.

Ahead of us, the sky was full of dark clouds trailing what looked to be thin curtains of mist.

Road said, "Storms coming."

"We going to be okay?"

"Yeah."

"You camp a lot?" I asked.

"I like to get away."

"From what?"

"Myself."

After almost an hour's drive, cutting through high mountains, Road took an exit marked

BAKERVILLE. NO SERVICES. We traveled along a two-lane road, not passing or being passed by anyone. The sky was gray. The trees around us were gigantic, the rocks high and close to the road. If there was a place called Bakerville, I never saw it.

After a few miles, Road slowed the truck and cut onto a narrow, bumpy dirt road. We bucked along for about half an hour, going deeper into dark forest. Hanging branches sometimes slapped us. As the truck jounced, the dream catcher flung about wildly, as if full of nightmares. I held on, wondering where we were headed. The dirt road came to an end. We stopped. Road turned off the motor. The deepest silence I ever heard took over.

I peered around. The world was mostly green, dark green. High above, treetops were swaying. Beyond the trees, I could see churning clouds. I said, "Where are we?"

"The best place. Nowhere. Roll up your windows."

Road got out, slamming the door behind him. He seemed to like the sound of leaving.

Having no idea what was happening, I reluctantly got out. The dirt lane had ended, but in front of us was a clearing maybe fifteen yards across. It was carpeted with grass, like a tiny park, or cemetery. In the middle was what appeared to be a circle of stones, surrounded by old logs. It reminded me of some ancient shrine we had studied in school, where they did human sacrifices. Wondering if Road had his pistol, I wished I wasn't alone with him.

As we got out of the truck, a thud of thunder came.

Road looked up. "It's a-coming." He pulled up one of the duffel bags, flung it over his shoulder, took up the other one by a cloth handle, and hurried into the clearing. "Come on!" he called.

I followed.

Once in the clearing he knelt down and began to pull sticks and cloth from one of the bags. Next he flung out a ground cover, then worked to set up a tent. Overhead, thunder banged. It grew darker. Treetops began to snap back and forth, like angry whips.

Not knowing what to do I sat on a log and watched Road work. When I saw the butt of Road's pistol sticking out of a side pocket, I knew I didn't want to share a tent with an angry man with a gun.

The sky got even darker. Thunder rocked and rolled. Rain started falling.

The tent was up. Road heaved the duffel bags into it and said, "Unless you want to get wet, you might as well get in." He held back a flap and crawled inside.

I hesitated, not wanting to go there with him. But when the rain began to pelt, I did. Surrounded by dim blue cloth, it was as if I had crawled into some kind of cocoon. I wiggled in only to have lightning crackle overhead like a series of pistol shots, enough to make me start. The tent fabric flickered with the light. Crashing thunder boomed. Rain beat down so hard I felt I was inside a drum.

Road tied the front flaps together. Then he sat back, clutching his knees. "We'll be dry," he said.

"Will it last long?" I asked.

"Never know," he said.

I sat there listening to the storm. Getting up my nerve, I said, "Why are we here?"

Road didn't answer. He just sat there, holding on to his knees, his Viet Vet cap pulled low, staring straight ahead. Of course, he knew I was there, and had heard my question. He didn't react.

I eyed the tent flaps, wondering if I should run away, bolt for the truck, and lock myself in.

Then, speaking softly, Road said, "You asked me how come your father and I don't get along. Well, as I see it, a man can't tell the truth until he gets to a safe place."

Overhead, lightning cracked and thunder burst. I flinched. "Is this safe?" I whispered.

"Just us against a God-made storm. Can't get safer than that."

I waited, feeling as if I was on the edge of something bad.

He took a deep breath. "How come your father and I don't get along? Long story short: Soon as I got out of high school—eighteen— not wanting to wait and be drafted, I joined the army. Get it over with. Before I did, I married my girlfriend, Nancy. She was seventeen. I was sent to 'Nam. Call it hell. Two tours.

"When I got out of the army, Nancy didn't know me. I didn't know Nancy. I didn't know myself. And when I got out, I didn't know my new kid, Mickey. Your father.

"By then, Nancy had had enough. She wanted a life. I didn't blame her. Divorce. I got full custody of your dad. Off she went. I didn't know where. Never saw her again. I doubt your father ever saw her, either. A few years back, I heard she died.

"I thought I could be a father. I couldn't. Only real thing were the nightmares, day and night. Let me tell you, the worst thing about having been to hell is you don't have words to describe it. Worse, it's trapped inside"—he touched his head—"like a car with its motor running, but you've locked yourself out, so it keeps going. Way I figure it, *words* are the keys that open the door. That's why I keep reading. Searching for the right words, the keys.

Maybe I'll find them. If I do, I'll get inside my head and turn that motor off.

"Point is, I was a lousy father. The worst. Too much anger. Drink. Other bad stuff. For your father's eighteenth birthday, he gave himself the best present ever. He took off. Left no word. I didn't know where he went. I don't blame him. I was—am—full of bad thoughts, bad actions, ghastly memories, and nightmares . . . always nightmares. What do they call it? Shell shock. These days, PTSD.

"Every few years your father and I pull the thin strings that still seem to connect us. Never completely cut. We hold on, but don't ask me what we're holding.

"You wanted to know *how come*. That's how come. I'm what you might call a casualty of war. And Mickey—your dad—he's one, too. Do you get on with him?"

"Not really."

"Then you're a casualty of war, too."

He became silent. Just sat there, holding his knees, rocking back and forth a bit. Outside, the storm went on, but it didn't seem as bad as the storm inside him.

I said, "Was the war *that* bad?"

"That's why I have so many dream catchers. Trying to keep the nightmares from coming at me."

"Do they work?"

"Still looking for one that will."

"What happened in the war?"

He was silent, and then said, without looking at me: "You really want to know?"

"Yeah."

Then he said what he had said before. "You look like Mickey when he was your age. He tried to get me to love him. Oh, yeah, he tried."

We sat there without talking. I had the sensation that the tent was its own world. We could have been in a cave deep in the earth. Or in a capsule shooting through space surrounded by nothingness.

Then Road began to talk. And he didn't stop. What he told me *was* astonishing. The fighting. The boredom. Friends he saved. Friends who saved him. Friends he lost. People he killed. Men, women, children. A lot was awful. A lot was brave. But all ghastly.

He went on and on. Sometimes I stopped listening. That didn't stop him from talking. Or looking at me. Sometimes I thought he was not talking to me, but to my father, telling him things he had never told him before. A few times, he even called me Mickey.

I never heard anyone talk so much. It was as if he hadn't talked for years and was making up for lost words. It was as if something inside of him was *making* words, and they came pouring out of him, like one of those snowmelt waterfalls.

The storm went. The sun came. We sat on the logs. I could see blue skies above the trees. He still talked. He built a fire. We had hot dogs, beans, packaged cookies. He kept talking. I had stopped listening a long time ago. It didn't matter. He kept talking. All day. That motor inside him never stopped.

It grew dark. I went into the woods to pee.

When I looked back, the electric lamp Road had turned on in the tent made it look like a lump of gold in the night.

I nodded off. Road led me into the tent, let me lie down, threw a blanket over me. As I fell asleep, I saw him through the open tent flaps, sitting by the fire, looking into the dwindling embers. For all I knew he was talking to the flames.

I slept.

When Road woke me in the morning, it was cold but bright. The grass had a coating of thin, white frost. When I breathed in, it was like drinking cold, clear water. He had a fire going. I sat down on one of the logs, and he handed me a cup of hot cocoa. He sat on a log opposite.

"You okay?" he asked.

"Stiff. You?"

"Good." Then he said, "I talk too much?"

"No."

"Pretty awful."

"I guess."

"You guess right."

I said, "Why do you have a pistol?"

"It's fake."

"What do you mean?"

"Walmart plastic. I figure it might scare someone off. I wouldn't trust myself with a real one."

"Who would you shoot?"

"Myself, probably. Come on, let's head back."

The next five days went fast. Something had changed in him. He was easier to be with. As if he really wanted to know, he asked lots of questions about me, my father, my mother.

We did things, too. The Colorado History Museum. A Rockies game at Coors Field, where the view of the mountains was better than the game. We rented bikes and went along what he called Cherry Creek, down to the Platte River where they once found gold, the gold that brought his ancestor to Colorado. He took me to a town called Marshall, and we rode horses. Mostly he talked. I tried to listen, but I'm not sure it mattered to him that I heard. What mattered to him was that he talked.

On Friday—two days before I was going to

leave—he told me he had that carpenter's job, replacing some steps for a guy he knew. He said he would be back in about six hours.

I knew exactly what I wanted to do. Soon as I was sure he was gone, I pulled a stool from the kitchen, climbed up, pulled down on that overhead noose in the hallway. The wooden steps came down silently.

I climbed up and found myself in a low storage attic. There were cardboard boxes piled up in complete disorder. The boxes seemed filled with junk, books, clothing, and papers. One box had been pulled forward, and was open. I had the impression someone had gone into it recently.

I looked inside. It was full of old photographs. I picked one up, and it showed Road, a young Road, standing next to a teenage-looking girl. He was in army uniform. She held a baby in her arms. My father, I was sure. Held by his mother, Nancy. RIP.

There were more pictures. Not many of the girl—Nancy, my grandmother—but plenty of my father. All ages of being a kid. One thing—in all those pictures, I never saw a smile on his face.

I pushed the box back to where it had been. I went down, and shoved the steps up. They closed up as slowly and silently as they had opened, steps to the past.

On Sunday morning, Road took me to the airport, and like my father had done, went to the gate with me. We sat there, waiting for the gate to open.

He said, "Thanks for all that listening."

"Yeah, sure." Then I said, "Can I come again?"

He looked at me, and actually smiled. "Any time." But it took him a moment to say, "Bring Mickey."

They called my flight. I stood up. So did Road. At the last moment, he reached into his pocket and pulled out a dream catcher.

"Hey, Paul, you know what? You're my dream catcher, and guess what—you work." When I took it, he gave me an awkward hug, as if he hadn't practiced much. I hugged him back, just as awkwardly.

"Glad you came," he whispered. And then he said, "Tell Mickey I love him. And you, too. Really."

KITCHEN TABLE

Billy Kinley had always dreamed of being a winner of the Staltonburg Memorial Day Bicycle Race. Racing was important to Billy because his father had been a stock car racer. But since his father took off when Billy was two, Billy didn't know much about him except what was tacked to the wall in his small room: a faded five-by-five glossy photo of his dad holding up a trophy he had won at a race somewhere. Right behind him was the car he had driven, a red Chevy with its name, Special Red, big and bold on the hood.

The marriage bust-up was not anything Billy's mom spoke about much. "He just left," she would say. That was all Billy knew about it, and there was kind of an understanding between him and his mom that he would not ask more. If he did happen to let something slip, the painful look on his mother's face warned Billy to move on.

Billy's mom loved Billy a lot. That said, he spent a fair amount of time without her around, because she worked weekdays as secretary at McManus Auto Body and Towing, then weekends clerking at the local Piggly Wiggly supermarket. She was trying hard to save money for the real house she so much wanted for the two of them. "Until then," as Billy's mom expressed it, they were living in a mobile home set in the middle of the Twenty-Third Avenue Trailer Park and Laundromat.

They often talked about the house they wanted to have someday—in particular, the kitchen. It was a bit of a joke with them. She wanted a small kitchen, with a small table nook, for just the two of them. *Cozy* was her word. Billy wanted something bigger, with an expandable table. "Just in case," he would say, looking away, "someone else came around for dinner."

As for the Memorial Day race, Billy's problem was that he didn't own a bike. His best friend, Joey, had one, and Billy had learned to ride a bike using it. Once, when Joey went to visit his grandmother in Iowa, he let Billy use the bike for a whole week. So he rode well, just didn't have his own bike.

The morning of his birthday, a Saturday, Billy slept in. When Billy woke, his mom led him into the small kitchen, her hand covering his eyes. Then she sang "Happy Birthday" slightly off-key and flicked away a sheet that covered something. It was a bike.

There wasn't a lot of money in the Kinley household. That meant the birthday bike was not exactly new, but had been purchased second-hand from Hank's New and Used Bike Shop on Vine Street. It didn't matter to Billy. The moment he saw that bike, he knew he was going to be the winner of the Memorial Day race, which was going to be held in a few weeks.

What's more, though he knew his mother did not—could not—go in for *big* gifts very often, this was a *big* gift. The bike store had done a fine job of refurbishing the bike, with its brand name (Specialized) in white on the crossbar, new tires, new seat, and new handle grips. The color—a splendid fire-engine red—was so shiny that nicks and scratches seemed minor, hardly worth noticing.

"It's your twelfth birthday," said his mom, and she hugged him so he couldn't see her tears. Even so, Billy knew they were there.

As Billy gazed at the bike, its red color, and the word *Specialized,* reminded him of his dad's car. He was about to tell his mom that, but checked himself. He did not want any hurt feelings, not that day.

"It's just what I wanted," he said, his grin as bright as an August sunflower. "I'm going to win the race for sure."

"Yours to have fun with and be responsible for," his mom said, proud to have made her son so happy.

An uneasy look came over Billy's face.

"Wasn't it very expensive?" he asked. He knew how hard his mother worked, how they were nibbling on the edge of being poor, that even so, bit by bit, she was saving for that house with the perfect kitchen.

"Billy, it's your *twelfth* birthday," his mother said.

"I know, but . . ."

"Tell you what," she said, guessing he needed some *reason* for his joy. "Your job isn't just to enter the bike race; you've got to win it."

Billy nodded in happy excitement. "First-place prize for kids my age is twenty-five bucks."

"Great," she said. "When you win it, you can put all that money into our house account at the bank."

"I can?" he said, delighted at the thought.

"I'm counting on it," she said earnestly, which suggested that was part of the deal.

"I'll do it," Billy promised. "And if I win, guess what?" he blurted out. "They'll put my picture in the paper. Maybe Dad will see it."

His mother said nothing.

Billy hardly ate his breakfast, but yanked on

his clothing and hauled his new bike outside. It was a beautiful spring day. Sun shining. A touch of easy breeze.

Billy insisted that his mother watch his first ride. He straddled the bike, touched fingers to the frame, bounced the seat, and checked the brakes. When he finally pushed off, he wobbled a bit, just enough to add an extra thrill to the moment. After a couple of seconds he found his balance, then shot around the trailer park, the smile on his face all the thanks his mother needed.

Billy—being Billy—said, "Mom, it's perfect. The best bike in the whole world. A winner. I love it. Thank you *so* much." He jumped off and gave his mother the biggest hug he could.

The rest of the morning, Billy rode his bike around, showing it off to neighbors, friends, and any kid he could. "I'm going to win the race, don't you think?" he said to everyone. Everyone agreed it was a fantastic bike. No one mentioned the nicks and scratches.

Around noon, when Billy finally got back home—his mother had gone off to her Saturday clerking job—he found a rag beneath the sink and worked to get the morning's dirt off the bike. He didn't just rub the frame down and scour the fenders; he cleaned every spoke.

Billy made himself a PBJ lunch and then went out with his friend Joey. The two of them went beyond the trailer park, on the old prairie meadow. Billy loved going fast, standing up on the pedals, swishing the bike from side to side, legs pumping like pistons, racing around all afternoon.

He did not win every race—Joey won some—but Billy won often enough to give him real hopes that come the Memorial Day bike race, he would win the real thing. "We still going to be best friends when I win the race?" he asked Joey.

Joey laughed. "I'm going to win it."

That night Billy cleaned the bike again, then dragged it into his small bedroom. It barely fit. He thanked his mother again, twice, and went to sleep—eyes on the bike—very happy.

That following week, when the bus dropped him home after school, Billy got his bike out of his room and raced around. When Saturday came, he registered for the Memorial Day bike race at Ace Hardware. When he did, he received a numbered Coca-Cola sponsored bib: D-87. Back home, he stood before the mirror in his mother's bedroom and looked at himself with the bib on, frontward, sideways, over his shoulder, grinning every moment.

Though he could hardly wait for the race, Billy knew he could use the three weeks to practice. So every day after school, hour by hour, he and Joey worked hard. It was not long before Billy was winning almost every time.

That Saturday night—two weeks before the big race—Billy asked his mom for permission to ride his bike to school on Monday.

His mom was not so sure.

"It's only three miles," Billy assured her. "Pete"—Pete was one of Billy's friends—"told me that. And guess what? He goes a back route that doesn't have much traffic. It'll be part of my training for the race. Mom, I have to win."

His mom became thoughtful. "It won't get stolen at school, will it?" she asked.

"Lots of kids bike to school," Billy assured

her. "That's why they have bike racks. And I want to show the other kids what a great bike you gave me."

There was some talk about getting a lock, but that was forgotten. Billy had not seen locks on other kids' bikes, and he didn't want to be a wimp or have his mother spend any more money.

Billy's mother drove the route Pete had suggested. It clocked out at 3.2 miles and seemed safe enough. She granted permission.

Sunday afternoon Billy cleaned his bike again until it glistened. He even asked for and received a dab of car wax from a neighbor so he could get the frame and chrome handlebars glowing.

As he worked over the bike, he realized he had already come to know its scratches like the lines in his palms. He told his mom they were part of his bike's personality. "Nobody's perfect," he told her with a look to some far-off place. "You have to learn to forgive."

His mother did not say anything, just smiled her sad smile.

It was a proud Billy who rode his bike to school on Monday. While in class, he left it with the other bikes behind the school, near the two bike racks the school had. They did not have enough slots for all the bikes, so lots of them were dumped on the ground. Billy would not do that to his bike. He leaned it carefully against a tree. Besides, the tree was in full leaf, so it shaded the bike from a too-hot sun.

When Billy got out of school, there it was, bright as a beacon. He was delighted to mount the saddle, and then he and Joey slap-scattered home, racing all the way.

On Wednesday, right after three o'clock dismissal, when Billy came to collect his bike, it was gone.

At first, Billy thought he had forgotten where he had left it, and went searching around the school. But as more and more kids claimed their bikes and took off, it became clear: his bike wasn't just gone; it had been stolen.

As Billy grasped what had happened, shock set in. Tears welling in his eyes, and a lot of pain in his chest, he kept roaming the school grounds, searching. Not finding it, he kept telling himself that maybe someone took it by mistake, that it would be brought back.

An hour later, finding it hard to breathe, Billy went into the school office and reported what had happened. The school secretary gave Billy a whole lot of sympathy, even as she said such things did happen.

Then she said, "I can't believe one of our kids took it. Did you have a lock on it?"

Billy admitted he didn't.

Then the secretary said, "Billy, why don't you go over to the district police station over on Fifteenth and report it. I'm told they find tons of bikes. Stolen bikes get dumped. Joyriding, I guess."

With a burst of hope, Billy ran all the way. He had been inside the police station once, the time Joey's dad filed an accident report.

The police station was small, a one-level building, with heavy glass doors. Bulletproof, kids said. Inside, it was a dreary place, one long room with a low ceiling. A couple of tables stuck out from one wall. Some faded posters hung about to remind people about safety at railway crossings and kids walking home from school.

At the end of the room was a counter, behind which a policeman sat talking on the phone. He had a weather-beaten face, a droopy mustache, a big belly, and half-closed eyes that suggested he never did get enough sleep.

When the policeman put the phone down, he said, "Hey, kid, how you doing? What's up?"

Billy came to the counter and said, "My bike got stolen."

"Uh-oh. When did this happen?"

"Today."

"Hey, I'm sorry. Where did you see it last?"

"At school. The Truman School."

"Locked?"

"No, sir," Billy said, small voiced.

"What's your name, son?"

"Billy Kinley."

"Tell you what, Billy Kinley," the policeman said. "I'll give you a form that you can fill out. You know, describe the bike. Do you know what kind it was?"

"A Specialized. All red. I got it for my

birthday. I'm going to race it in the Memorial Day race, and I got to win. Like my dad."

"Well, get your dad to help fill out this form. Did the bike have an identification number on it?"

Billy didn't want to say that his dad wasn't around.

The policeman, not understanding why Billy hadn't replied, said, "They sometimes put those numbers under the crossbar."

"I don't think it's there."

The policeman pulled a long face. "Sorry to tell you, Billy, but it's hard to prove a bike stolen without that ID number. Come on over here. Let me show you something."

He led Billy back behind the building to a small fenced-in area. Some fifteen bikes were stuffed inside.

"These are bikes we picked up," the policeman explained. "You know, stolen or lost. You're welcome to look, but if yours just got taken, it's not likely there. Not yet. Why don't you come back tomorrow and check? And bring that form.

But, like I said, without an ID number, it's going to be hard to prove any bike is yours."

That evening Billy told his mom what had happened. She was as upset as he was.

Billy, elbows on the small kitchen table, head cradled in his hands, the form in front of him, said, "I went to the police and they gave this to me. Said my dad should help fill it out."

His mom said, "Suppose I could do it, don't you think?"

"Suppose."

"Hey, let's hop in the car first. Maybe we can spot your bike around town."

Billy and his mom cruised the neighborhood, going by Billy's school, driving in and out of streets. For an hour and a half, they searched but saw nothing of the bike. Only darkness made them quit.

"I'll tell you one thing," Billy said with a sigh.

"What's that?" his mother asked.

"Just because we can't see it doesn't mean it's not somewhere. Has to be."

His mom patted his hand. "I guess that's true."

When they got home, his mom helped Billy fill out the police form. "Wish we knew the bike's number," she said.

Billy said, "I know all its nicks and scratches. If I saw it, I'd know it was mine."

Next day, right after school, Billy brought the filled-in form to the police station. The same police officer took it. "You're welcome to check out back again."

Billy did, but his bike was not there.

With the Memorial Day race coming up soon, Billy was not ready to give up. Each day when school let out, he hurried to the police station to see if his bike had been found. He went so often, the desk officer came to know him pretty well. But the bike did not show up.

Once he left the police station, Billy went searching, wandering over a lot of the town before heading home. He liked to be there when his mom got back from work.

It was on Friday, just a few days before the big race on Monday, when Billy found his bike.

He was on Alameda Street when a boy went whipping by on a bike. In a flash, Billy realized it was *his* bike. "Hey!" he yelled.

When the kid did not halt, Billy ran after him, calling, "Stop! Stop!"

The kid on the bike slammed on the brakes.

Billy, almost out of breath, caught up with him. The kid was a teenager, a short chunky boy, with a fat face and wisp of mustache along with a shock of floppy sandy-colored hair. He wore baggy jeans and a white T-shirt. On his bulging left arm was a tattoo, an American eagle. Billy had never seen him before.

"What do you want?" the teenager said to Billy.

Billy was eyeing the bike, checking out the nicks and scratches he knew so well, making sure it was his. No doubt about it. It was. He said, "That's my bike."

The teenager grimaced and said, "Says who?"

"It's mine," Billy insisted. "You stole it from my school. The Truman School."

The teenager dumped a whole bucket of cuss words on Billy.

Billy stood there, taking it without a blink. But when the teenager was done, Billy said again, "You stole it."

"Prove it," the kid said.

"Got a V-shaped scratch on the inside of the rear fender," Billy shot back. "Go on, dare you to look. Double dare you."

Now it was the teenager who said, "It's mine."

"Give it back," Billy said, and put his hand on the handlebar. The kid knocked the hand off.

"It was my birthday present," Billy shouted, all red-faced. "I was going to be in the Memorial Day race. It's going to make me a winner. Anyway, it's too small for you. Give it back!"

"It ain't yours, and *I'm* going to win the race," the older kid said, shifting the bike away. He lifted his foot onto the pedal, prepared to take off.

"I'll call the police," Billy screamed, balling his fists, eyes full of tears. "Give it back!"

The teenager slammed his foot down on the pedal, so that the bike shot off like a rocket.

Billy raced after him. "Thief! Thief!" he yelled. He got to the end of the block and took the turn the kid had taken, only to find he had disappeared.

Boiling with fury, Billy searched one street after another. Both thief and bike were gone.

Billy tore over to the police station. When he got there, he had to wait in line. First, there was a couple who were having an argument. Then there was an old man reporting that his Social Security check was missing.

When Billy finally got up to the desk, it was the same desk officer he had spoken to before.

"Hey, Billy. Got some news?" the policeman asked.

"Some kid on Alameda Street has it."

"Good for you!" The policeman reached for a pad and pencil. "What's the kid's name?"

"Don't know."

"Where's he live?"

"Don't know that, neither."

The policeman put down his pencil. "Hey, Billy, I thought you said you found it."

Billy said, "The kid who stole it was on the street. Riding it. I told him to give it back, but he just cussed me and took off."

"Where'd he go?"

"Don't know."

The officer sighed and leaned over the counter, elbows down, hands clasped, and said, "Billy, there's not much we can do about it if we don't know who took it, or where it is."

"But I can't win without it," Billy cried. "And the race is in three days!"

"Tell me about it. I'm the finish-line judge. Look, I'll put in a call. Can you describe the kid who had it?"

Billy did the best he could. He told about the white T-shirt. The tattoo.

"Where was the tattoo?"

"On his left arm. An American eagle."

"That's useful," the policeman said. "We'll try." He did not sound hopeful.

"I've got to get it back," Billy pleaded.

The officer turned to the police call box and in a loud voice began to alert the town's two squad cars.

When Billy reached home, his mom was there. Full of fury, he told his tale. His mom said, "Come on. Get in the car. We'll go look."

They searched, focusing on the area where Billy had seen the teenager with his bike. There was no sign of the boy or the bike.

"Maybe when you found him, you made him nervous," Billy's mother said as they drove slowly home. "Made him so nervous, he dumped the bike, and the cops will pick it up now."

Billy stared out the window. "I got to get it to win," he said.

Come Saturday and Sunday, Billy spent all of his time roaming Staltonburg. He checked in with the police station three times. By this time, the desk officer greeted him like an old friend.

"Hey, kid," the policeman called to him as Billy, long-faced and sad, walked by after checking the bike cage yet again. "Come on over here."

"Yes, sir."

The policeman clasped his big hands together and leaned forward. "Look here, son. I don't think your bike is going to show up. And

I know you want to be in the race tomorrow, right?"

"I really need to win."

The officer lowered his voice, and leaned forward. "Okay, now what I'm suggesting," he said, "isn't exactly dotting the i's and crossing the t's. I'm just saying you *could* go into the bike cage, find yourself a bike. Then you *could* tell me it's the one you lost, and I *could* sign it over to you. After a few months, when no one claims them, we sell 'em anyway."

Billy did not say anything.

"And if you didn't want to do that," the policeman continued, "you could, you know, just *borrow* it, and then bring it back after the race. Am I making myself clear?"

Billy shook his head. "I only want to race my bike," he said. "It's the winner."

"Okay, kid," the officer said. "Just trying to help."

"Thank you, sir," said Billy. Feeling desperate, but not knowing what to do, he dragged himself home.

* * *

Memorial Day proved to be glorious. The sky was deep blue with a few fluffy clouds moving along like lazy sheep, the air as mellow as warm pancake syrup. Trees were dressed up in leafy green. Lilacs were in bloom, along with some lilies and even some early roses.

The Staltonburg Memorial Day Parade always took place along Market Street. It formed up at the corner of Rochester and Elm at ten a.m. sharp. In the lead was the Boy Scout honor guard, two Eagle Scouts who carried the national and state flags. Soldiers with white rifles flanked them. There were Cub Scouts and Brownie outriders, beating out a snappy marching rhythm on small snare drums. The drums were held over their stomachs with red, white, and blue sashes.

Lots of other town groups marched by, from the Veterans of Foreign Wars, to the Friends of the Library.

At the wag-end of the parade came the kids on their bikes, from toddlers on tricycles and tiny two-wheelers with training wheels, on up to the older kids.

Billy—with his Coca-Cola racing bib on— watched from the sidewalk along with his mother, looking for his red bike. He and his mom had worked out a plan of action. Billy had remembered the teenager saying he intended to be in the race. If he saw him or his bike, he would tell his mom. Parade or no parade, she promised she would wade right in and do what she had to do to get Billy's bike back.

Trouble was, Billy didn't see his bike. Twice, he thought he did. Once he even called, "Mom!" False alarm. The parade went by without any incident. Or Billy's bike.

"Maybe," Billy's mother suggested, "he's afraid you'll see him, so he won't be in the race."

Billy shook his head and said, "That bike's a winner."

"Come on," his mother said. "Let's watch the races."

The races, run by the police and fire departments, were held in the Piggly Wiggly parking lot where portable bleachers had been set up. On the far right, a starting line had been marked off with bright orange road cones. A policeman with a pistol that shot blanks stood by.

At the far other end of the lot was the finish line, marked by more cones. Standing by that line as judge was Billy's friend, the policeman. A card table was set in front of the bleachers with a bunch of shiny plastic trophies lined up for the winners. Each trophy held an envelope with twenty-five dollars in cash. A reporter from the *Staltonburg Defender* hovered around to take pictures of the winners.

Billy and his mother found themselves some seats in the stands, up high, so they could see everything.

"If you see that boy," Billy's mom said, "just point him out. No fighting."

First up were the toddlers on their tricycles. Just as many girls as boys. When the starting gun went off, some of the little kids were so scared they just sat there and cried—which brought laughter. One kid went the wrong way. A red-faced little girl crossed the finish line, kept going, and had to be hauled back to be told that she'd won. She looked bewildered and happy at the same time.

The races went on, one after the other, gradually working their way up the age ladder. After each race, the finish line was adjusted so the course became longer. Billy, increasingly tense, watched intently.

When they got to the twelve-year-old level — Billy's race — he stood up, straining for some sign, *any* sign, of his bike. His mother, just as anxious, stood right there with him, hand on his shoulder.

They didn't see a thing.

Some other kid — Billy had never heard of him — won. His pal Joey came in second. Billy slumped a bit, but insisted on standing, watching.

The final race was for the teenagers. There were many kids, all jumbled up around the starting line. It was mostly boys, though a couple of girls joined in.

"If he's coming at all, he'll be there now," Billy heard his mom say. Billy had already had that thought.

The policeman lifted his pistol and fired a blank to start the race.

At first, the racers were bunched up, so it was hard to see who was in the lead. Bit by bit the pack stretched out and the leaders settled in.

That's when Billy screamed, "There it is!" and pointed.

His mother looked. In the lead was the short chunky boy, pedaling furiously on a red bike that was too small for him.

"That's him. That's my bike!" Billy kept screaming. "It's winning!" He scrambled down from the stands, his mother right behind him, trying to keep up by saying, "Excuse me, please. Sorry," as she worked her way through.

By the time they got down to the ground Billy's red bike had zipped across the finish line — first. The kid riding it lifted both arms high over his head as if he had scored a touchdown.

Billy tore after him.

The teenager had spun the bike around and was facing in. Billy's friend, the police officer, was at the finish line. He was moving toward the winner, hand extended for congratulations. So was the photographer. That's when the police-man noticed Billy charging across the lot. The teenager saw him, too. He spun the bike around and took off. If he moved fast when he was racing, he was doing double time getting away. No picture was taken.

Billy, trying to catch the thief, kept running after him. Not that he could catch him. Within seconds, the teenager was gone. With the bike.

The policeman, who had seen the whole thing, figured out the situation right away. "Was that your bike?" he asked Billy. "Was that him?"

"Yes, sir," Billy gasped. "It was."

The policeman took a step in the direction the thief had taken, but seeing how useless it was, he stopped. "He's gone," he said.

"But—but my bike . . ."

"It's gone, too, Billy."

The look on Billy's face said something to the policeman.

"Follow me," he said.

He started walking back along the course. Billy followed, as did his mom, who had caught up.

The policeman reached the trophy table. He beckoned Billy over. "We got some kind of a tricky thing here," the officer said to the fire chief, who was sitting behind the table. "The winner of the last race was riding a stolen bike. The bike belongs to this kid. I can vouch for that."

The fire chief looked at Billy, then at the policeman. "What am I supposed to do?" he asked.

The policeman said, "The bike won, didn't it? You should give the trophy to this boy."

Billy spoke right up. And what he said was, "I don't want it."

"Hey, kid," the policeman said. "Your bike won. So you won." He looked at Billy's mother, trying to get *her* to do something.

Billy's mom just stood there. She didn't know what to do.

"I didn't win!" cried Billy, and ran off.

The cop picked up the trophy. "Are you his mom?" he asked.

Billy's mom nodded.

The officer did not offer the money, but he

did hold out the trophy. After a moment, she took it.

Back at the mobile home, Billy's mom found him on his bed, one hand behind his head, the other holding the picture of his father.

"You won the trophy," she said, holding it up.

Not wanting to show his mother his pain, Billy rolled over so she could not see his face. "Just because I can't see Dad," he said, "doesn't mean he's not somewhere. Has to be. You don't understand," he cried. "The bike was the winner. Not me. He'll never find me, because you're not a winner unless your picture is in the paper."

Billy's mom stood there, gazing down at her boy. For just a second she considered reaching out and taking the picture away. Instead, she sat down on the bed by his side, stroked Billy's hair, and said, "Billy, you've convinced me. The kitchen table in our house does need to be bigger. Just in case someone shows up for dinner."

BEAT UP

I stood in front of my bathroom mirror brushing my hair, but I wasn't paying much attention. I was thinking about the dance that night at St. George Episcopal Church. The dance, run for neighborhood kids by our church, was held four times a year. Anyone between the ages of thirteen and eighteen could go as long as they did not smoke, drink, use drugs, or make trouble. I had no interest in any of that, but, uneasy about going, I brushed my hair this way, that way, ten different ways, never getting it right. It would have helped to have looked.

Whenever my school had a class party or a dance, I went. They were easy. I knew the kids, knew the chaperones, and knew how it all worked. I felt comfortable. I could — and did — have a great time. The dance at St. George would be different. I had never gone before. A live band was promised, so a big crowd was expected. My classmates didn't usually go, so I would probably know only a few kids.

The reason I was going was that Alice Rollack suggested I come. I liked her a lot. Not that I had ever told her. As far as she was concerned, we were just friends. I wanted it to be more. During the past week, we had talked in school, and she said she was going to the church dance with a bunch of her girlfriends. "Why don't you come?" she said.

Feeling as though she had asked me out — I'm sure I blushed — I promised to go. But when I told my best friend, Arlo, that I was going to the St. George dance and suggested we go together, Arlo shook his head. "No way I'm going," he said.

"Why?"

"Lot of rough stuff at those dances."

I felt instant alarm. "Like what?"

"Like gangs."

"Gangs?" I said to Arlo, my stomach churning. "That true?"

"Hey, buddy, would I lie?"

I never thought of myself as particularly brave. When it came to things like fighting, or any kind of violence, I shrank from it. Just the thought of it made me tense. Not that I ever told anyone. Not even Arlo. I was convinced that if people found out, they would think less of me. At the same time, I have to admit, fighting, rough stuff, was not part of my life. Now there was Alice, the dance, my promise that I would go—and Arlo's warning.

Which is why I went to the kitchen where my mom was preparing dinner. As casually as I could, I said, "Thought I'd go to the dance at St. George tonight."

"That's nice."

"But . . . I don't know if I should."

"Why's that?"

"Arlo said there might be gangs."

Mom paused in her work to look around with anxious eyes. "That doesn't sound so great. Better talk to your dad. He'll be home soon."

Dad always gave me good advice. That wasn't only because he was a successful trial lawyer whom people called constantly for guidance. Or that—as he often told me—he was the head of the family, with the responsibility to solve complications and organize us all. Or even that he had been a champion boxer at Michigan State University. I admired him for all of those things, but also because when I went to him, he mostly made me feel like he was there to help.

Mostly, but not always. Because there was something about him that scared me. Don't get me wrong. I wasn't scared he would hurt me physically. He didn't and wouldn't. My fear was that he would think poorly of me, consider me in some way a failure. Not up to his mark.

He was a big man, six foot three, and broad chested. His wide shoulders were thrust forward, adding to a powerful presence. His face was swarthy so that even though he would shave in the morning, he'd shave again if he and Mom went out. His eyebrows were dark and craggy, too, which gave him a fierce appearance—an appearance, he claimed, that helped him in the courtroom. "You have to dominate," he once told me.

People who saw Dad and me side-by-side often said I looked like him. There was the same dark complexion, the same heavyset body, the same pale, gray eyes. They also said—because of my large feet—that I would be bigger than he was. Sometimes when I'd look into my mirror, I'd see his face in my face. I liked that, but as far as wanting to *be* another Dad, with all that bigness and strength, though I thought it would be great, I didn't think it was likely. That was also something that troubled me, not that I ever spoke about it.

That night, shortly after six, Dad got home from work. It being Friday, he sat in his big chair, jacket off, shirt collar open, tie askew and pulled down, drink in hand. That's when I approached him.

"What's up, Charlie?" he said. "You look troubled."

Unsure how to explain my uneasiness, and not certain how he would take it, I became anxious. "It's about a dance, at St. George," I began. "Tonight."

"Sounds good to me."

"Well, I was thinking of going. But . . . they said there might be gangs there."

"Gangs at a dance?" Dad repeated. "At our church?" He had a habit of repeating information, a way—he once told me—that allowed him, when in court, to take a little time so as to think out the strongest response.

"Yes, sir."

"How many . . . gangs?"

"Don't know. One. Two."

Dad smiled his I-know-the-answer-before-you-ask-the-question smile. "Charlie, try to be precise. A sloppy mind makes the world sloppy. Now, how *many* gangs?"

Flustered, I said, "Maybe one."

"*Maybe* one. Is this fact, rumor, gossip? Who told you?"

"Who told me? Ah . . . kids."

Those big eyebrows of his went up. That smile again. "Someone in particular?"

"Well . . . Arlo."

"Ah, Arlo."

His *ah* made me wince. Dad was not impressed by Arlo. "All I can say about Arlo," he once told me, "is: it's smarter to have smart friends."

Sure enough, Dad said, "How does Arlo know?"

I shrugged.

"Has he *been* to one of these dances?"

"Don't think so," I admitted. Long ago, I had learned to be truthful to Dad. He could catch out a lie the way Sherlock Holmes detected clues. Dad had brought me to court a few times, so I could see him in action. Now, as if he were addressing a witness, he jabbed a finger toward me. "So Arlo doesn't know for certain about this. He wasn't actually there."

Not wanting to reveal any more about my nervousness, I just said, "No, sir. I guess he doesn't really know."

Dad smiled again. "You want to go to the dance, don't you?"

"Yes, sir."

"Charlie, what you're saying is that there's a risk, a small risk that something unpleasant might happen."

"Yes, sir."

"You know," said Dad, his fist punching the air like the boxer he once was, "everything in life is a risk. Is that going to keep you home? What's important is how you put up a fight. Win some, lose some. Remember my boxing trophy? Wasn't easy. Trust me, I took some knocks. You know our family motto: Biderbiks don't cry."

"Yes, sir."

"My advice, Charlie: go to the dance." He reached into his pocket, drew out a neatly folded wad of bills, and peeled off a new five-dollar bill. "Have fun."

"Yes, sir."

I went to the dance. Everything went fine. I had a good time hanging around Alice.

When the dance ended, Father Mark, the minister — a short, round fellow who dressed in black, save for his white clerical collar—smiled and shook everyone's hand as we left.

Alice—and her girlfriends—were all going to sleep at her house. Her mother's car was going to be so full of giggling girls, there was no room for me to be driven home.

"I can walk," I said.

"Thanks for coming," Alice said with a nice smile, which made me feel great. The girls piled into the car, and with a friendly wave, I started to walk home, pleased with myself and glad I'd taken Dad's advice.

St. George was located on Montague Street, maybe fifteen city blocks from my home. Even at that hour—ten o'clock—the street was busy. There were restaurants, cafés, a bookstore, a food market, all of which were open. Looking at all the people, I felt connected and walked relaxed, almost jaunty.

Reaching the end of Montague, I turned onto Willow Street, where my home was. Willow was totally different from Montague: narrow, old, with no stores, just ancient three-story brownstone houses where people lived.

Street lamps—ornamented with wrought-iron curlicues—shed weak, wavering light. The tightly parked cars, long, low, and lumpish, seemed abandoned. A few spindly trees, their leaves brittle and brown, cast lacelike shadows on pavement made of irregular cracked slate. After the raucous music and the crowded dancing, the street seemed deserted and extra silent. As I walked, I heard my own footsteps.

I thought I was the only one on the street until I heard a whistle, low but distinct, like the call of a solitary bird. It seemed to come from behind.

I paid it no mind until I heard a second whistle. This one came from in front. When yet another came from right across the street, I stopped and tried to see who was there.

It was too shadowy to see anything. But when another whistle came, my heart began to race. Something was going on, something not good.

I was four blocks from home. I could run it easily, but I didn't want to overreact, jump at nothing. I stood there and listened intently.

Another whistle. This one also came from behind, but closer. Darting a glance over my shoulder, I began to walk fast, but halted when a new whistle came from in front of me. Then a whistle came from the right side of the street. Peering into the darkness, I thought I saw someone crouching behind a car.

I wanted to run, but didn't. I was too scared to know what to do.

Simultaneously, whistles came from three sides. In the gloom, I saw three boys coming toward me. Then more. Since they kept to the shadows, I couldn't tell how many. Next moment, I realized I was surrounded, and it was too late to run. I stood there, heart hammering, finding it hard to breathe.

"Hey, kid," a voice called.

I spun toward the voice. Right near me, a tall, gangly teenager stepped out from behind a car. I had never seen him before. He wore a black leather jacket with silver studs along the sleeves, which, despite the dim light, gleamed. The sleeves were too short so that his hands dangled white, ghost-like. Then he held up his right hand, fist toward me, a kind of salute, so I could see his knuckles. He had blue tattooed letters that spelled out H-A-T-E.

No matter which way I looked, more boys came out of the darkness. Maybe a dozen. They walked slowly toward me, sauntering. As my stomach knotted and I panted for breath, I recognized one or two of them from the dance. Some were tall. A few were short. Some had sideburns. One or two appeared younger than the others. Two had lit cigarettes in their mouths, the burning ends glowing red. Forming a circle around me, they stood staring, nobody speaking, nobody smiling. In all my thirteen years, I had never been so frightened.

"Hey, kid, enjoy the dance?"

I peered around to see who had spoken.

"Over here, kid."

I turned. It was the boy in the studded black jacket. His face was narrow, his eyes small.

"Hey, kid," he said, "I asked you if you enjoyed the dance."

"Wh-what?" I stammered.

"The kid's a moron," someone else said. Others laughed. The laughter sounded forced.

"I'm asking, you have a good time at the dance?"

"Yes," I managed to say.

"Got any money on you?"

I reached a hand into a pocket, took out a dollar bill and a few coins. "That's all," I said, my palm up.

Someone stepped forward and snatched the money away. Two coins fell to the sidewalk, making tinny sounds. Automatically, I bent toward them.

"Leave 'em!" the boy snapped. "They ain't yours anymore."

I stood up.

"Hey, kid—what's your name?"

"Ch-Charlie."

"Okay, Charlie boy. You want out of this circle, you're going to have to fight one of us."

I felt as if I were sinking into a vat of cement. "What?" I said, though I had heard perfectly well.

"Said you're going to have to fight one of us."

My stomach clenched. Dad's words— *What's important is how you put up a fight*—went through my mind. I tried to curl my fingers into a fist, but I was too panicky to do more than lift my arms. Instead, I asked, "Why?"

"The kid asks why."

The others boys laughed. That time it sounded real.

"When you go to St. George, you have to pay your dues. Fighting is your dues."

"I—I don't want to fight."

"Hey, Charlie boy, you don't have a choice. Look around. Fight who you want. Go on. Take the smallest. Don't matter. Hey, Pinky, you're the smallest. You fight him."

One of the boys—he *was* smaller than the others—moved out of the circle toward me. His fisted hands were up. He was grinning.

I shook my head. "I don't want to fight," I said, and began to back up.

The small boy kept advancing, prancing,

smirking, jabbing the air with his fists, like a boxer entering the ring.

I retreated farther, only to bump into the boys behind me. Their hands shoved me back toward the center. The small boy darted forward and punched me in the face.

Without thinking, I put up one hand to protect myself and swung out wildly with my other arm. I didn't hit anything.

Next moment, I felt a blow on my head. Exploding lights filled my eyes even as my legs buckled. I fell to the ground. For a small moment, I lost consciousness. When I opened my eyes, I saw feet all around me. Afraid to move, I kept still, shut my eyes. I heard: "You hit him too hard, idiot! You could have killed him."

"He's okay."

I felt a sharp kick on my leg, but remained motionless. I told myself: *Stay still. If they think I'm hurt, maybe they'll go away.*

Sure enough, someone said, "Hey, he must be really busted."

"Let's get out of here," one of the kids called.

There was the sound of feet running, followed by silence.

I lay on the cold slate, not moving, eyes still closed, wanting to be sure they had gone. I peeked up. Seeing no one, I lifted my head and looked around. They were no longer there.

I pushed myself onto my feet. There was some dizziness. My head and leg were sore. Limping, sniffling, I began to run for home, constantly looking over my shoulder.

When I reached home, I was too shaky to use my key. Instead, I pushed the doorbell. It was my mother—in her purple bathrobe—who opened the door. I almost fell into the house, my sense of relief, and safety, enormous.

"What's the matter?" Mom said. "What happened?"

I pushed past her and went into the living room. Dad was sitting in his easy chair, newspaper in hand. He looked up.

Almost choking, I cried, "I got beat up," and collapsed onto the couch.

Mom, arms extended, started to move toward me. Changing her mind, stifling a cry, she rushed to the bathroom and returned with a damp cloth.

Dad leaned over me. "You all right?"

I nodded. As Mom wiped dirt from my face and forehead, I felt my panic subside.

"What happened?" Dad asked.

Haltingly, beneath the intent eyes of Mom and Dad, I told them.

When I was done, Mom said, "Let me check your eyes for a concussion." She studied me, then backed away, saying, "They're okay." Hovering between tears and fury, she said, "I'm going to call the police."

Dad said, "Don't waste your time. It's too late for them to do anything."

All the same, Mom reached for the phone.

"Molly," Dad barked, "leave it!"

"People should know," she objected, but did not touch the phone.

Dad pulled up a chair so he could be close to where I was. "Now," he said, leaning forward, "how many did you say there were?"

I covered my face with my hands and sniffed. "I'm not sure. Maybe twelve."

"Not sure. Maybe twelve. A dozen. And how many did they say you had to fight?"

There was something in Dad's voice that made me take my hands from my face and look at him. He was gazing at me, fiercely. I turned away. "Ah . . . one."

"One. Look at me," Dad snapped. "You said *one*. And what did you do?"

I forced myself to look into Dad's eyes. What I saw was anger. I said, "I, you know, kept asking them why I had to fight."

"You've already told me that," Dad said, irritation in his voice. "I asked you what you *did*."

"Nothing. I was too scared."

"Too scared," Dad echoed. In his voice I heard mockery.

I said, "Then . . . they—they hit me. From behind. I think it was with a stick." I put a hand to the bump on my head as if to prove it. "And when I just lay there, they thought they killed me or something. So I stayed there."

"You just *stayed* there," repeated Dad. His scorn was stronger.

"So they would leave me alone," I said. A wave of nausea swept through me. I turned away.

Mom said, "Ted, I think it would be a good idea for Charlie to get some sleep. He's been hit on the head. We can deal with this in the morning. Sweetheart," she said to me, "do you want a snack before bed?"

"A sandwich." I started to get up.

Dad held out a hand, preventing me from moving. "Wait a minute. I need to make sure I understood. Do I have it right? You just *lay* there? *Pretending* you were hurt?"

Hearing contempt in Dad's voice, I was filled with shame. "Uh-huh," I murmured.

"Why?"

"Told you," I said, struggling to keep back tears. "I thought if I got up, they would have . . . you know . . . knocked me down again. Hurt me worse."

"Charlie, did you ever consider that you might have put up *some* fight? Did you?"

"Dad," I whispered. "There . . . were a lot of them."

"You just told me you only had to fight *one*."

Mom hurried up with a sandwich on a plate as well as a glass of warm milk. "Ted, for God's sake, leave the boy alone. He's not in court. He's been hurt. Frightened."

Dad, backing away, picked up his newspaper. He stood there, looking at me fiercely. Then he rolled the newspaper, slapped the palm of his open hand twice, took one more frowning look at me, and stalked out of the room.

Though I knew the answer, I said, "What's bothering him?"

"He's upset for you; that's all."

I looked at the doorway through which Dad had left. "He's ashamed of me," I said, the pain in my chest awful. "For not fighting."

"Don't be silly. I think you should eat a little something." She brushed hair out of my face. "I'm glad you're okay. What a terrible thing. It must have been very frightening."

"Yeah," I said, pulling away from her. I bit into the sandwich. It was tasteless, but I kept eating. As I ate, I kept watching the door in hopes that Dad would come back. Same time, I was scared he would.

He didn't.

When I woke the next morning, I had a headache. Reaching up, I felt the spot at the back of my head. The swelling was down.

I lay quietly. It felt good to be in bed. Safe. Eyes closed, I thought through what had happened last night. I told myself I didn't care what Dad said. I was glad I had not fought. They might have killed me.

All the same, nervous about what Dad would say, I was reluctant to get out of bed. I looked at the clock. It was almost nine. Late. I made myself get up, pulled on jeans and a white T-shirt, and headed for the kitchen, treading lightly.

A note was on the fridge door: *Doing errands.* Clean dishes were in the drying rack. The morning newspaper lay on the counter. It had been read. I was relieved that my parents weren't there.

I was making up my mind what to have for breakfast when the house phone rang. "'Lo."

"Hi, Charlie! This is Jane." Jane was my mother's best friend.

"'Lo," I said, bracing for the worst.

"Oh, Charlie, your mother told me what happened last night. I am *so* sorry. Are you all right?"

"Yeah, sure. Fine."

"Thank goodness. You read about these things, and then it happens to someone you care about. Makes me so upset. I'm so relieved you're fine."

"Thanks. Mom is out."

"That's okay. It's you I wanted to talk to. Charlie, I'm so glad you were not badly hurt."

I made myself a breakfast of bacon and eggs; sorted the newspaper; found the sports section; and, since it was Saturday, looked to see what football games were being played.

The phone rang again.

"'Lo."

"Charlie! Hey, how are you, buddy? Uncle

Jess! Your mom told me what happened. You doing okay?"

"Yeah, sure."

"Good for you. Hey, don't let it get you down. I'm telling you, cities. You should move up here. Nothing like that here."

"I might."

"You do that."

"Want me to tell Mom you called?"

"Naw. Already spoke to her. It was you I wanted to talk to. Hang in there, buddy! You'll be fine! Love you!"

Before I had finished breakfast, I heard from two more of Mom's friends. Both asked if I was feeling all right. The calls made me feel good. People cared about me.

Then Arlo called. "How was the dance?"

I told him what happened both during the dance and after.

"Oh, man, told you stuff like that happens there," Arlo said. "You couldn't drag me to one of those dances. I like living too much. But you're okay, right?"

"Right."

We talked and made plans to meet later in the day.

The last call was from Alice. "Oh, my God," she said. "Arlo called and told me. Are you okay?"

"Sure."

"I feel so bad. Wish we had given you a ride."

"No, really, I'm okay. Thanks for calling."

"See you in school."

I felt good.

I was cleaning up my breakfast dishes when my parents returned.

"Morning, sweetheart," said Mom. "How you feeling?"

"Fine." I glanced at Dad. He was silent. His look was glum.

"Does your head hurt?" Mom asked.

"Not really," I said. "There were a bunch of calls."

Dad just stood there, but Mom looked around.

I listed the callers. I did not mention Arlo.

Mom said, "What did they want?"

"They were . . . asking about me. I guess you told them about last night." I kept stealing looks at Dad, watching his reactions.

"People need to know," said Mom.

"Yeah," I said, turning to Dad. "But how come they were all calling?"

Dad looked around sharply. His face was ashen, his eyes cold. "They wanted to know how you avoided a fight," he said, and marched out of the kitchen.

Stunned, I stared after him.

Mom came up to me and held my arm. "Oh, Charlie, he didn't mean anything. He's just—"

Shrugging her off, I said, "He thinks I'm a coward, doesn't he?"

"Of course he doesn't. He's just very concerned about the whole thing. He's your dad. He feels he has to do something."

"Do what?"

"I really don't know."

I bolted from the kitchen, went to my room, slammed the door, and threw myself on my unmade bed. Hands under my head, eyes shut, I replayed what had happened the night before.

It made me shudder. Then I thought of Dad's reaction and remembered his motto: Biderbiks don't cry. Wiping my tears away, I felt humiliated, betrayed, beat up all over again.

"I'm not a coward," I said, staring at myself in my mirror. "I'm not. They would have killed me." My anger began to swell. Seeing Dad's face in the mirror image, I spun away, made a fist, and punched the wall. I hurt my hand, but the pain in my hand was less than the pain in my heart.

Over the next few days, our place was tense. And silent. No one talked about what had happened. Dad avoided me. I avoided Dad. I was afraid to say what I was thinking. But the following Tuesday, during dinner, Dad announced that he had arranged a meeting that would be held on Thursday at St. George. "I'm going to do something about these gangs," he informed Mom and me.

"Like what?" I asked, feeling uneasy.

Ignoring my question, Dad turned to Mom. "I'd like you to call as many families as you know. Charlie's friends, classmates. Tell them about the meeting. I intend to use this incident to organize parents. They should bring their teenage boys. We have to make sure things like this don't happen again."

"Things like what?" I demanded, certain Dad was referring to my *not* fighting.

Dad gave me a cold glance, but only said, "Father Mark, the church minister, has agreed to cooperate. He doesn't have much choice. I told him the church had to bear some responsibility for what happened. Potential legal consequences. These dances have to have better security. At my suggestion, one of the things he agreed to do is hold boxing lessons for boys. Apparently, there's a small gym in the church rectory basement. Perfect place."

"Boxing lessons?" I said incredulously.

"Right. Twice a week. Seven thirty. Till nine. You start next week. I've arranged for a good young teacher."

"But I don't want to. I—I don't like fighting."

"Charlie, my boy, you don't have a choice."

"Don't you care how I feel?"

"Frankly, no. Charlie, the meeting is going to

happen and you're going to be there—like it or not. And you'll be taking those classes. I will not have a son who won't fight back. If you're going to get through life, you need to learn how."

I bolted from the table, went into my room, and slammed the door shut.

For the millionth time, I went over what happened that night and the next day. How my dad had reacted. How I felt. I thought about the calls that had come. They hadn't criticized me. But over and over again, I heard Dad's words, *They want to know how you avoided a fight.*

"I'm not a coward," I said aloud. "I'm not."

Then, like an echo in my head, I heard the words: *Prove it.*

It took time, but I decided what I'd do.

The meeting Dad arranged was held in the rectory building next to St. George. It was a long, rectangular room, the walls painted blue, with portraits of ministers in colorful robes hanging in a row. Some twenty parents were in attendance, along with their sons. Everybody sat in folding chairs.

When I came into the room with Dad and

Mom, I glanced around to see who was there. To my horror, I saw kids I knew. Briefly, they stared at me, and then averted their gaze. I was already edgy, but seeing them made things worse. I focused on the floor, and reminded myself what I was going to do.

Dad, Mom, and I sat in the front row.

Father Mark stood up. The idle chatter hushed.

"Good evening," he began in his mellow voice, hands folded before him. "May God's grace touch you all. My name is Father Mark, and I welcome you all to St. George. I only regret that it took an unfortunate incident to bring some of you here."

I clenched my teeth, and murmured, "Do it," under my breath.

"However," continued the minister, "at St. George we have a great desire—a commitment— to be part of the neighborhood. Anything we can do to contribute to the peace and well-being of the neighborhood and its young people has our wholehearted support.

"Now, I would like to call upon Mr.

Biderbik—who was kind enough to organize this gathering—to speak."

Dad went forward. I stayed with Mom. I was sure I could feel the eyes of everyone in the room on my back. I clasped my fingers tightly, all the while glancing at Dad, my anger building. *Do it.*

Looking confidant and comfortable, Dad looked around the room. He smiled. "Good evening. My name is Theodore Biderbik, a parent. I have an apartment on Willow Street. That's my wife, Molly, and my son, Charlie, in the front row. This is our church.

"I want to thank Father Mark for welcoming us here. And you for coming. This meeting has been called to protect our children. After the last dance at the church, there was an unfortunate incident in which my son was set upon by a gang. He had been at the dance. When walking home, some fifteen, twenty young men assaulted him. Though my boy put up a heroic resistance, there were too many of them to—"

Heart beating wildly, I stood up. All faces turned toward me.

Dad, looking puzzled, said, "Charlie, I am talking."

"That's—that's not what happened," I said, struggling to get out the words.

"Charlie!" Dad barked.

Mom pulled at me. "Charlie!" she whispered. I stepped away from her grasp.

"What happened," I continued, my voice growing stronger, my eyes fixed on Dad, "is that these . . . twelve guys surrounded me. Twelve."

"Sit down!" Dad cried.

"They told me I had to fight one of them. Any one. Even the smallest. But I was too scared. See, I was . . . very frightened. So when one of them hit me, I just lay there . . . hoping they would go away. And they did. Then I ran home."

The room had become absolutely still.

I turned to face the crowd. "But—but my dad . . . he thinks I was a coward. He thinks I should have fought. It doesn't matter to him that I was scared. That I could . . . have been hurt. Badly. Killed, maybe. That's why my dad called this meeting. It's not to protect the neighborhood. It's because my dad is ashamed of me, his son. This meeting is for him. He's afraid people will think badly of him. Because of me. But I think he's just interested in himself. So I think he's . . . the coward."

I shifted back toward Dad. He was staring at me as if I were a stranger. And though he opened his mouth, no words came out.

THE AMALFI DUO

As always, Gramps was waiting for Marco to come out of school. "How you doing?" he called as Marco, heavy book bag on his back, ambled out of the school doors into the cold January air. A boy was with him.

"Hi, Gramps," Marco said. "This is Nicky, my new friend."

"Pleased to meet you," said Gramps. He held out his hand. Surprised, Nicky shook it.

Marco said, "He just got shifted into my class." Marco was in sixth grade.

Without asking, only saying, "Hey, let me have that," Gramps eased the heavy book bag off Marco's back and slung it over his own shoulders.

"Somebody meeting you?" Gramps asked Nicky.

"I walk home by myself," said Nicky.

Marco eyed Gramps to see how he would receive that information.

All Gramps said was, "Well, Marco's mom or dad drives him to school every morning, and I pick him up from school and walk him home. Since Marco's parents work late a lot, Marco and I often have dinner, just the two of us. We're sort of like Batman and Robin."

"Oh," said Nicky.

"What do your parents do?" asked Gramps.

"My dad is a programmer. My mother is a musician."

"No kidding? What does she play?"

"She gives recorder lessons and plays the saxophone in a brass band."

"Saxophone," said Gramps. "It was invented

by a Belgian, Adolphe Sax. The 1840s, I think. Isn't that great? Someone inventing a musical instrument, and they named it after him."

Marco turned to Nicky. "Gramps knows everything."

"Pretty much," Gramps said good-naturedly.

Nicky eyed Gramps.

"He was in the Korean War," Marco explained. "Then a sailor, and went around the world a few times. Then a cowboy and a teacher. When my grandmother died, he moved in with us. My parents made our garage into an apartment. It's full of books, and he reads all the time."

"And I share everything I learn with Marco," added Gramps. "My only grandchild. You have grandparents?"

"They live far away."

"Too bad," said Gramps. "Well, learn anything interesting today?" he asked Marco. To Nicky, he said, "Marco and I play this game walking home from school. He quizzes me about something he learned in class to see if I know it." To Marco, he said, "Come on, let's show him. Ask me something." Even as he asked his question, he took Marco's hand in his.

Marco thought for a moment. As he did, he pretended to have an itch on his ear and freed his hand from Gramps's hold. Then he said, "What mineral is there more of than anything else in the world?"

"Carbon. Am I right?"

"Yup."

"See what I mean?" Gramps said to Nicky. To Marco he said, "Go on; ask me another."

Marco glanced at Nicky and then said, "Do you know how Thomas Jefferson became president?"

"Easy. Back in 1800, the early days of the United States, there was a tied presidential vote between guys named Aaron Burr and Thomas Jefferson. The vote went to the House of Representatives. It took thirty-six votes before Jefferson became president. Burr became vice president."

Gramps laughed. "See? He never stumps me."

Nicky said, "Must be hard knowing so much."

"Hey, like Marco said, I've been around. And there's no substitute for experience. Marco's lucky I can share it with him. It'll give him a head start."

Nicky stopped at the corner. "I go this way."

Marco said, "See ya!"

Gramps said, "Nice meeting you."

As Marco watched Nicky walk off, Gramps said, "I feel sorry for your new friend. Every kid needs a grandparent like me to hang around. Got another question?"

Marco shook his head. For the rest of the way home, Gramps chatted about what he had read that day.

As they stepped into their home, Marco said, "Can Nicky come over after school tomorrow?"

"Sure. Give him a call. But I'll need to speak to his mother. Let me tell you something," said Gramps. "Music is perhaps the highest form of art. It's universal. But I have to admit," he went on, "though I've done a lot of things, I've never learned to play an instrument."

"I thought you could," Marco said, taking his backpack and heading for his room.

"Oh, guitar a bit, but not much," Gramps called after him. "Something I picked up in the sixties. Like everyone."

Marco reappeared, basketball in his hands. "You could do it," he said. "If you wanted to."

Gramps laughed. "You're probably right," he allowed. "I have to admit, I'm always good at what I do. How about you? Would you like to play music?"

"Drums."

"Not real music. Just beats. Oh. Your mother called. It'll be just you and me for dinner."

"Okay." Marco said. "I'm going next door."

"Basketball with Carter?"

"Yeah."

"Dress warm. And just so you know: Wilt Chamberlain holds the record for most points in an NBA game. One hundred. That was way back in 1962."

"Nice," said Marco as he went out the door.

"Dinner at five thirty!" Gramps shouted

after him. "Chicken Marengo. The recipe was invented by Napoleon's Italian chef on the Marengo battlefield."

Marco had already gone.

Gramps and Marco had dinner in the kitchen. The chicken was served with noodles. While they ate, Mr. Amalfi shared a cookbook with pictures of all different kinds of pasta.

Marco, remembering Nicky's question, turned from gazing at the mosaic of noodles on the page to Gramps. "Is it hard knowing so much?"

"You kidding? I love it. And I love sharing what I know with you."

"How come you quit being a teacher?"

"Had to. Turned sixty-five."

Marco said nothing.

"Want to know why sixty-five?"

"Okay," Marco said automatically.

"The idea of retirement was first developed during the nineteenth century in Germany under Chancellor Bismarck. He chose the age. Probably because in those days not many people lived to be that old. The age—sixty-five—sort of got stuck. Doesn't mean anything. Look at me. I could go on forever."

"Probably," Marco agreed.

It was after dinner when Gramps said, "Hey, go call that Nicky about coming over tomorrow. If he says yes, let me speak to his mother. What's Nicky's last name?"

"Pelescue."

"Sounds Romanian. Got its name because it used to be a Roman province during the days of the Roman Empire."

Marco called Nicky, and the boys agreed to get together after school the next day. Then Gramps got on the line and worked out the details with Nicky's mother. But he spent most of the time talking to her about music and the lessons she gave.

When he got off the phone, he said to Marco, "It's all set. Nicky can come here after school. I'll drive him home."

"Thanks." Marco was doing his math homework.

"Nicky's mother is very interesting," said Gramps. "Like your friend said, she plays lots of instruments and gives lessons. Mostly the recorder, to kids. But to grown-ups, too."

"I think it'd be more fun to be a drummer."

"You should learn real music first."

Marco continued to work on his math.

"Hey, Marco," said Gramps after a while. "Here's an idea: if you took recorder lessons first, you know, learn to read music, play a real instrument, then I'd get you drumming lessons."

"You would?"

"Mean it. What do you think? Hey, I'd take lessons, too. We could practice together. When we played, we could call ourselves the Amalfi Duo. How's that sound?"

"You'd be much better than me."

"Well, sure," said Gramps. "But you could try."

Marco did another math question, then looked up. "If I took lessons and just did okay, could I still do drums?"

"You know me. I keep my word."

Marco considered. "I'll do it," he said. "As long as you don't mind that I won't be as good as you."

When Marco's dad got home, Marco was in bed reading. His dad looked in and asked him how his day was. Marco told him about Nicky, his new friend. Then he said, "Dad, how come Gramps is always telling me things?"

Marco's dad laughed. "I know; he's like those people who keep leaving flyers at our door. You keep telling them you don't want any more, but they keep coming. It's just the way he is. Always has been."

"Wish he'd stop."

"Good luck. I've tried."

His dad kissed him on the top of his head and said, "Don't stay up too late reading." He headed for the door.

"Dad," Marco called. "Could I walk home from school by myself?"

"What about Gramps?"

"I'm older than Nicky is, but he walks home alone."

"I'll talk it over with your mom when she gets home, okay? Sleep well!"

The next day after school, Nicky came over to Marco's house. For the most part, they stayed in Marco's room, playing video games.

Now and again, Gramps would look in. Once he said, "You guys have any idea when television was invented?"

Nicky said nothing. Marco said, "When?"

"Nineteen twenty-seven. That's even older than me."

Ten minutes later Gramps was back. "What about the first video game. Know when *that* was?"

The boys, intent on their game, said nothing.

"Nineteen fifty-eight," said Gramps. "*Tennis for Two*. Invented by a guy named Higinbotham. First game I remember was called *Pong*." He retreated.

Nicky, while playing, said, "Does your grandfather ever stop telling you things?"

Marco shook his head.

"Would drive me nuts."

"He does," said Marco.

"Can't you get him to stop?"

Marco focused on the video game.

When Gramps drove Nicky home, he made arrangements with Nicky's mother for recorder lessons for himself and Marco. The first was scheduled for the following Thursday at four o'clock.

"Here comes the Amalfi Duo!" Gramps proclaimed as he drove back home. "*Duo*. Italian word for two. Sounds lovely. *Duo*."

That evening Marco asked his mother about walking home from school alone. "We talked it over, Dad, me, and Gramps. Gramps thinks you should be a little older."

"Aren't you and Dad in charge?"

His mom smiled. "Well, walking home with you means a lot to Gramps. Hey, I love the idea that you're going to take recorder lessons with him. Whose idea was that?"

"Gramps."

"Is that something you really want to do?"

"He said if I learned to read music, he'd get me drumming lessons."

"Sounds like a good plan," said his mom.

On the following Thursday Gramps and Marco presented themselves to Mrs. Pelescue with plastic alto recorders and Steckheart's *First Recorder Book* in hand.

Mrs. Pelescue was a slight woman with a dark complexion and large, brown eyes. Her thick black hair was arranged in a single long braid down her back. She greeted Marco warmly. Nicky was there, too, and he waved to Marco. Marco grinned.

"Marco!" said Mrs. Pelescue. "Welcome. Nicky has told me all about you. And Mr. Amalfi. You are most welcome, too. Do come in."

"Call me Gramps, the way everyone does."

Mrs. Pelescue smiled. "Doesn't seem respectful," she said, and led them to her living room, a room whose walls were covered with framed drawings, paintings, and photographs. Directly off this area was a large alcove. On the walls of the alcove hung a great variety of instruments. There were recorders of all shapes and sizes, as well as a saxophone. In the center of this relatively small area were three straight-backed chairs with music stands.

"Here's where we work," Mrs. Pelescue told them cheerfully as she urged her new students to sit side by side. She turned to Nicky, who was looking on. "Lesson time," she said.

"See ya," Nicky called, and retreated.

"Now then," said Mrs. Pelescue, "Marco and Mr. Amalfi, we'd best begin."

"We're the Amalfi Duo," said Gramps.

Mrs. Pelescue laughed. "Wonderful!" Then she briskly informed Marco and Gramps of her expectations: she took music seriously, and wanted as much from them—which meant at least a half hour of practice every day. "But beyond all else," she said, "music should be a lovely experience, one that brings joy, not just to those who play but to those who hear it. Music is for sharing. Now, listen."

She put a large wooden recorder to her lips and poured out a woody cascade of lilting music that was, by turns, passionate, soulful, and frolicsome. "That's from Bach's Suite in A Minor," she explained when she was done. "Did you like it?"

Gramps turned to Marco. "The composer's

full name was Johann Sebastian Bach. Eighteenth century, German. Great harmonies. And guess what? Twenty children."

Marco, saying nothing, looked at Mrs. Pelescue.

"Ah, you know your Bach," she said to Gramps. "What did you think, Marco?"

"I like it," he said.

"Now," said Mrs. Pelescue, "about the recorder. It—"

Gramps interrupted: "Didn't become popular in Europe until the fifteenth century."

"Goodness, you do know a great deal about music."

Marco studied the floor.

Mrs. Pelescue placed sheets of music paper marked with basic scales on the music stands, then showed them the proper fingering for three notes. "Not the tips of your fingers, but the fleshy part so as to cover the holes completely." She then explained the right way to put the recorder to the lips and blow.

"This way." She demonstrated, sounding a clear, firm tone. "Marco, let's start with you."

Marco lifted his recorder to his mouth and blew. The sound came out squeaky.

"Good start, but—look how my lips and tongue work." Mrs. Pelescue demonstrated anew. "All right, Marco, again."

Marco made a second try. That time his tone was firm.

"Excellent!" Mrs. Pelescue cried. "A quick learner. Now, Mr. Amalfi," she urged. "You try."

Gramps lifted the recorder to his lips and blew. The sound was shrill.

"Try it this way," Mrs. Pelescue suggested.

Gramps made a second attempt. If anything, an even stranger sound resulted.

"Again, please," she said with a smile. "It does take some practice."

No improvement.

"Marco. Show your grandfather."

Marco blew into the recorder. His sound was good.

"First rate!" Mrs. Pelescue cried. "Mr. Amalfi, watch the way Marco does it."

Gramps frowned but paid close attention

as Marco gave a demonstration. Then Gramps tried, but he continued to have difficulties.

Mrs. Pelescue smiled patiently and explained once more, focusing on Mr. Amalfi.

When the hour-long lesson was over, Mrs. Pelescue complimented them both and gave instructions about practicing.

"Remember," she said, smiling but playfully shaking a finger at them, "a half an hour of practice each day. But the Amalfi Duo has begun."

"What do you think?" Gramps asked Marco as they walked home.

"She's nice," Marco said.

"You sure got the hang of it fast," said Gramps.

"Don't worry. You'll be better than I am soon."

"Probably," Gramps agreed.

Over the next week, the Amalfi Duo practiced faithfully. Marco quickly mastered the first assignment. Out of boredom with simple scales, he taught himself a few extra notes, and then went on to learn the first tune in their music book. His tone was even. His finger work was smooth. What he played sounded melodic.

As for Gramps, no matter how much he practiced — and he worked much more than the half an hour a day that was suggested — his tone remained erratic, hesitant. He became so frustrated, he purchased a second book, *Teach Yourself the Recorder,* and worked with that, too.

Marco, who listened and watched Gramps struggle, said nothing.

At the second lesson, Mrs. Pelescue called upon the duo to show her what they had achieved that week. Marco played first.

"Well done, Marco!" Mrs. Pelescue exclaimed. "I'm *really* impressed. You have a natural talent. Now, Mr. Amalfi, let's hear what you have accomplished."

Gramps was not nearly as good as Marco, so Mrs. Pelescue had to correct his fingering and help him with his blowing technique. As the lesson progressed, she spent more time with him than with Marco.

Over the next three weeks of lessons and practicing, Marco advanced rapidly, whereas Gramps, though he did get a little better, lagged far behind.

One day in school during lunch, Nicky said to Marco, "My mother told my father that you're a natural musician."

"She did?"

"Said you had real talent."

"What about my grandfather?"

"Said you were better. You said he knows everything. Well, trust me, he doesn't know how to make music."

At the end of the fifth lesson, Mrs. Pelescue said, "I have been thinking. While I do believe it's quite wonderful that the two of you want to play together, perhaps each of you would make better progress if you had separate lessons. Of course, you'll come at the same time, one half-hour lesson after the other. That way," she said with care, "you could go at your own pace. What do you think?"

Marco looked at Gramps.

"Mr. Amalfi?"

Gramps frowned. "I don't think so. The idea was that Marco and I would be the Amalfi Duo."

Mrs. Pelescue pursed her lips. "In time, perhaps. All in good time. As for separate lessons, well, for now, let's hold off."

"What do you think of Mrs. Pelescue now?" Gramps said as he and Marco walked home from the lesson.

"I really like her."

"I find her impatient," said Gramps. "And I'm not always sure I understand her instructions. Do you?"

"We could take separate lessons," said Marco.

"Hey," said Gramps, "we're supposed to be the Amalfi Duo."

That week Gramps made the decision—which he carried out faithfully—of practicing two hours a day. He did this in his own apartment when Marco was at school. As for Marco, not only did he do his required half an hour; he too put in some extra time.

Gramps said, "How come you're practicing more? You don't need to."

Marco said, "I like playing."

"I'm sticking to half an hour a day," Gramps said.

At the lesson the following Thursday, Mrs. Pelescue said, "Bravo, Marco!" when he played his assigned Mozart. "I can tell you've been working really hard. A natural. You need to move on to even more sophisticated music."

Then, when Gramps played his piece, a rather simple French folk song, she said, "Well, Mr. Amalfi, that certainly shows *some* improvement. But—here I must push you just a little bit—if you could find a way to practice just a *little* more . . . perhaps an extra fifteen minutes a day, I assure you, you would make even greater progress. Do you think you could try to do that?"

"I'll try," Gramps said grimly.

It was the following Monday afternoon, when Marco and Gramps were walking home from school, that Gramps said, "We haven't played our fact game for a while."

Marco sighed, then said, "Who was president when the First World War began?"

"Wilson," said Gramps. "Admit it. I know American history backward and forward."

Marco glanced up at Gramps, but said nothing.

Then Gramps said, "Mind carrying your own backpack? I'm a little tired today."

That night, when Gramps had gone to a talk at the local library, Marco called Mrs. Pelescue. "I was sort of thinking that you were right. Gramps and I should have separate lessons. I'd like to get good, and he, you know, sort of slows me down."

"I think you're right," she said.

"Only thing: you have to tell him. If I say anything, he'll get upset."

"I won't say a word."

By the end of the following week, it was agreed — with urging from Mrs. Pelescue — that Marco and Mr. Amalfi would take separate lessons.

"Do you mind the separate lessons?" Marco asked his grandfather as they walked home from school.

"Not at all," Gramps snapped. "Only for a while. Until I catch my stride."

Marco said, "I'm glad you suggested lessons. I really like them."

Gramps continued to practice at least two hours daily when Marco was at school. He played from a book Mrs. Pelescue had suggested: *Popular Broadway Tunes for the Recorder.* With all his hard work, he did get better, though he had trouble keeping the proper tempo. Fortunately, Mrs. Pelescue had an extra metronome and was willing to lend it to Gramps. It helped, a little. As for his finger work, that continued to be clumsy.

Marco worked extra hard, too, practicing a Brahms sonata that was as lovely as it was difficult. Whenever the boy played the haunting melody, it brought real emotion to Gramps.

"Why do you get all worked up when I play that?" Marco asked him.

"Why do you think?" Gramps replied. "Because it's nice."

When they walked home from school,

Gramps insisted they play their fact game. What's more, he rapped out his answers and then added comments like, "See? I knew it," or, "Bet you didn't think I'd know that one, did you?"

"No substitute for experience," said Marco.

"Don't you forget it," said Gramps.

In May Mrs. Pelescue announced that it was time to decide on the piece they would be playing for her students' annual June recital.

Marco's response was "Could I play that piece you had me listen to the other day?"

"That's Samuel Barber's Adagio," she said. "It's harder than it sounds, but it pleases me that you want to do it. It's very beautiful."

When she asked Gramps to consider a piece for the recital, he became silent and then said, "Who is going to be there?"

"The usual. My pupils and their parents. It's quite a lovely occasion. You know, Mr. Amalfi, it's what I think music is really about, a shared experience."

Gramps said, "Will any other adults perform?"

"Other than you, Mr. Amalfi, I don't have any other adults taking lessons."

"I'll have to think about it," Mr. Amalfi said glumly.

It was while the whole family was at dinner that Marco mentioned the recital. He wanted his parents to be there and told them what he was going to play.

"The Amalfi Duo's debut," exclaimed Marco's mom with delight.

"What are you going to play?" Marco's dad asked Gramps.

Gramps scowled. "I'm not sure I'm going to."

"How come?" Marco's mom asked.

Gramps studied the food on his plate, rolling over a carrot with his fork. "It seems to me," he said, "that music—my music, anyway—is a private thing."

At school the next day, when Marco was eating lunch with Nicky, Nicky said, "I heard you and your grandpa play the other day during your lessons. He's so bad. But you know what? You're good."

At dinner that night, Marco's mom asked Gramps about the recital. "Have you made up your mind about playing?"

"Don't know yet."

"You should," said Marco.

"Why?" demanded Gramps.

Marco said, "You heard what Mrs. Pelescue said. 'Music is for sharing.'"

"I like that," his mom agreed.

"Come on, Dad," Marco's father said to Gramps. "Marco's right. And we really want to hear the Amalfi Duo."

"We'll see," was all Gramps said.

The next day Marco listened as his grandfather practiced "Memory."

"I thought of doing it for the recital, but it doesn't sound right," Gramps complained.

Marco said, "Sounds good to me."

"Really think so?" He looked at Marco hard.

Marco turned away. "Yeah, I do."

"Well, Mr. Amalfi," Mrs. Pelescue asked him at the end of the next lesson, "have you made up your mind about playing in our recital?"

"When is it?"

"One week from Thursday."

"I'm certainly getting a lot of pressure to play."

"From who?"

"Marco."

"Mr. Amalfi, you do realize how unusually talented Marco is, don't you?"

"Probably gets his talent from me," Gramps said. He was staring glumly at the floor.

"You have gotten better." Then she added, "Considering where you began."

At dinner — it was just Marco and Gramps — Gramps said, "You really think I should play at that recital?"

"Yup."

"Why?"

"This was your idea. That we'd play together. The Amalfi Duo."

Gramps frowned. "We're not actually playing together. But, maybe. One condition."

"What's that?"

"Your mom and dad can't be there."

"Why?"

"Needs to be just people involved in music."

"But—"

"I'd feel better about it."

"Okay."

"Then I'll do it."

The recital was scheduled in one week's time, four o'clock on a Thursday afternoon.

As soon as Marco went to school, Gramps practiced. As for Marco, he told Gramps that after school he was going over to the park to shoot baskets. Once there, he found an isolated bench and practiced his recital piece.

The day of the recital came.

"Are you nervous?" Gramps asked Marco as they approached the Pelescue house. He was wearing a suit. Marco had on a white shirt with one of his father's ties. The collar was a bit big, and made him look smaller than he was.

"Not really," Marco said. "You?"

"Experience has to count for something," Gramps said, and used a handkerchief to wipe the sweat from his forehead.

When Marco and Gramps arrived at Mrs. Pelescue's, recorders in hand, her other students were already there. They were all young people, ranging in age from six to fourteen. Most of the kids had brought along at least one parent, though one girl came with her babysitter. Everyone was dressed up. The boys wore neckties. The girls wore dresses.

When Marco came in, Nicky sidled up to him and whispered into his ear. "My mom says it'll be okay if we play football in the yard after refreshments are served."

"Cool," said Marco.

Mrs. Pelescue had arranged twenty-four folding chairs so that they all faced the alcove. She ushered her students into the front seats. The parents and Nicky sat behind.

Mrs. Pelescue stood before the group.

"This is always a special occasion," she said, her hands clasped before her, a warm smile on her lips. "As I always tell my students, playing music together is the *essence* of music. Of life, if I may say so. You students have all worked very hard. All of you have something to share. I'm proud of you.

"Now, I think we will start with Virginia Woodly. Ginny and I have been working together for two years. Ginny, will you come up and play for us?"

The girl stood and took her seat before the music stand.

Mrs. Pelescue placed some music on it, then bent over and whispered, "Tell the audience what you will be playing, dear."

Virginia looked up and blushed. "I am going to play Corelli's Sonata in D Minor," she said breathlessly.

With solemn silence, the people in the room gazed at Virginia.

Putting her recorder to her lips, Virginia played with a touch of nervousness, missing one or two notes. But as she played, she gained confidence. The audience listened intently, respectfully. When she finished, there was warm applause.

"Good job, Ginny!" Mrs. Pelescue enthused.

One by one, she introduced the rest of her students. While some played better than others did, all played with great conviction. The audience was generous with its response.

Then there were just Marco and Gramps left to play.

"The next musician, Marco Amalfi, is a new student this year. While he has not been playing for very long, he plays with very real talent. Marco?"

Marco stood and took his place on the performance chair. He looked up and caught Nicky's eye. Nicky winked at him. Marco grinned back. Then he looked at Gramps. He was sitting very still, his face pale.

Marco, composing himself, said, "I'm going to play Samuel Barber's Adagio for Strings, as transposed for recorder."

He began to play, quickly capturing the deep, slow, and intense passion of the music. The room seemed to swell with painful emotion. The small audience, taken by surprise, listened raptly.

When he had finished, Marco lowered the recorder. For a moment, the audience, caught up in the power of the music, remained silent. Then they applauded enthusiastically.

A beaming Mrs. Pelescue stood up. "Isn't that wonderful!" she exclaimed. "Just a few months of study." Impulsively she gave Marco a hug. "A natural musician.

"Now," she said, "we have a special treat. When Marco came to study with me, he was part of a duo. The Amalfi Duo, they call themselves. His grandfather, Mr. Amalfi, decided to study with me too. What a brave thing it is when someone his age is willing to try something new. So, Mr. Amalfi, if you please."

Gramps, recorder in hand, stood up. Stumbling a bit, he came forward on shaky legs. He took the chair as Mrs. Pelescue placed his music on the stand before him.

Gramps pressed his hands together. They were trembling. Mouth dry, he tried to swallow and then licked his lips. Though he knew he needed to begin, he could not move.

"Mr. Amalfi," Mrs. Pelescue said in a stage whisper, "would you tell us what you'll be playing?"

Gramps looked up.

"Well, ah," he began, "it's called 'Memory,'

by Andrew Lloyd Webber. From the musical *Cats*."

Hands unsteady, Gramps lifted his recorder to his dry lips. He licked them once, twice, scrutinized the music, and started to play. His fingers seemed to have a life of their own. A clumsy life. The notes squeaked, slurred, tumbled. Though horrified by what he was hearing, he made himself go on.

Mrs. Pelescue stepped forward and gently placed a hand on his shoulder. "Mr. Amalfi," she whispered gently, "why don't you stop and try again?"

Gramps stopped playing. Breathing deeply, he looked out at the audience. Everyone in the room, faces absolutely devoid of emotion, was staring at him. Tension filled the room. Mr. Amalfi looked at Marco. The boy was staring at him, too, his face blank.

Summoning his strength, Gramps started to play again. This time, the music came a little easier, but with his hands still wobbly, it was often off-key, constantly on the edge of going out of control. Twice, he felt compelled to stop and breathe deeply, but forced himself to go on. When he played the final note and knew he was done, he was drained, exhausted.

The audience offered polite, embarrassed applause.

Mrs. Pelescue came to the front. Her hand rested on Gramps's shoulder. "Thank you, Mr. Amalfi. That's our final performance. I do appreciate all of you for coming. I think it's been a splendid afternoon of music. And again, I congratulate all of our young musicians. And you too, Mr. Amalfi," she added with a nervous laugh. "Now, there are refreshments in the kitchen."

Students and audience moved away. Gramps remained in his performance chair. Marco stayed in his chair, too. Alone in the room, the two looked at each other.

"I stank, right?" Gramps asked Marco.

Marco nodded.

Gramps said, "Anytime you want drumming lessons, let me know."

Marco was silent for a moment and then said, "I think I'll stay with the recorder. I like it."

GOING HOME

How come I get to spend only one weekend a month with Dad?" demanded Damon. He was sitting on the couch watching an action movie on the small TV.

His mother was standing in the doorway of the TV room. "We've discussed this before, many times," she said.

"How about an answer?" said Damon, his eyes on the TV, not on her.

His mother gave a small sigh before saying, "I try very hard not to be critical of your father. I don't think it's helpful."

"You can say what you want," said Damon.

"The divorce settlement was worked out by both your father and me."

"Why just one weekend?"

"That's all I could get him to agree to."

Damon, eyes still on the screen, was silent for a moment before he said, "I don't believe you."

"Ask him."

"I know some kids who spend half a week with their moms, half with their dads."

"I'm sure that's true. But that's not the way your father wanted things."

"Why wasn't I consulted?"

"You are still a minor, but you are welcome to talk with him about it."

"If he says I can, will you change things?"

"I'm open to whatever is good for you. And once you are sixteen, you can work out your own living arrangement."

"That's four more years."

"You get an A for arithmetic. It would be nice if you did as well in school."

Damon said nothing.

His mother said, "I'll drop you off tomorrow morning. I'll pick you up on Sunday at six o'clock."

Damon finally looked at her. "I've decided to live with him — in my real home — full-time. Be with you one weekend a month. See how you like it."

She waited a moment before saying, "I guess that's an option."

"He'll agree."

"Damon, this is your home."

"I hate living with you . . . and Adam."

"So you've told me many times."

"Why did he have to move in?"

"He's my boyfriend. We love each other. He and I wanted to live together."

"You're too *old* to have a *boyfriend*. 'Who's that?' my friends ask. 'My mom's *boyfriend*.' It's embarrassing."

"Do you want me to call your father and remind him you're coming?"

"Why would you think he'd forget?"

"When was the last time you talked to him?"

"None of your business. What are you doing this weekend?"

"Adam and I are going to paint the kitchen cabinets. If you like, we can wait until next weekend, so you can help with the painting."

"I'll be at Dad's house. It's my home!" Damon shouted. "It's where I should be. Don't pick me up on Sunday. I'm not coming back!" Using the remote to flick off the movie, he fell back on the couch, clasped his hands over his stomach, and closed his eyes.

His mother waited a few moments and then retreated.

Saturday morning, at eight thirty-two, Damon's mother drove her car up to the curb in front of her former husband's house. Damon, sitting next to her, had his gym bag on his lap. He had stuffed in as many clothes as he could. His backpack, filled with his schoolbooks, was on the floor between his feet.

He looked at his watch and said, "You're two minutes late."

"Sorry."

Damon studied the car in front of them, a shiny new Toyota Land Cruiser. "You should get a car like that," he said.

"I can't afford it."

Damon looked at his father's house. He had lived in it from the time he was born until a year and a half ago, when his parents divorced.

It was a two-story brick structure, with a deep front porch. The gray-shingled roof came down over the porch like a peaked cap pulled low. The front door was painted a dark blue. A large spruce tree was planted to one side of the small lawn. A couple of dandelions had popped up, their yellow petals already beginning to wilt.

The style of house was called *bungalow* for reasons Damon did not know. His father, who sold houses, told him the word, but didn't know where the name came from, either.

At least the house stays the same, Damon told himself. The thought made him feel good. His dad had also told him that when he died, the house would go to Damon.

A thought popped into Damon's head: *What*

if Dad suddenly died—now? Would I get the house right away? Could I live here alone? Or at sixteen? Don't be stupid, he told himself.

There were similar-looking houses up and down the block, all of which had been built years ago. Damon liked it that neither the street nor houses seemed to change.

His mother said, "You okay?"

"I mean it," he said. "I'm staying with Dad."

"I suggest you talk it over with him first. Then, if that's what you work out, have him call me."

"You don't believe me, do you?"

"If you need me, Adam and I will be home all weekend. Do you have your cell phone?"

"I don't need you. And Adam is your boy-friend, not mine."

His mother reached out and touched Damon's hand. He jerked it away. She said, "Say hello to your father. Love you."

Damon put his hand on the door latch but didn't pull the handle. *I'm doing it,* he told himself. Even then, he sat for another moment before saying, "I'll be home for a weekend in a month."

When his mother said nothing, Damon shoved the car door open. Gym bag clutched in one hand, backpack in the other, he swiveled out of the car and staggered to his feet. Then he kicked the car door shut behind him and headed up the cement slab walkway toward the house. He made sure he didn't look back.

One slab had a crack across it. The crack had been there for as long as Damon could remember. From spring on, a few blades of grass—and sometimes a dandelion—grew in the crack. Damon remembered something from when he was very young: "Step on the crack; break the Devil's back." Careful not to squash the dandelion, he stepped on the crack.

He glanced back toward his mother. Her car had not moved. She was watching him. "Go!" he shouted with a surge of anger.

His mother put the car into noisy gear and drove off.

Damon watched the car move down the

street. *I'm doing it,* he told himself again. Feeling excitement, he turned toward the house.

Three concrete steps, painted brown, led up to the porch. Damon noted the chipped brick near the doorway. When he was three, he had taken a hammer to the brick; it was another reminder that the house never changed.

He did notice that the lawn in front of the house was cut neatly. Usually, when he came over, his dad asked him to cut the lawn. Maybe his dad *had* forgotten he was coming over.

Don't be stupid, he told himself a second time.

He went on the porch. At the far end was a swinging couch with canvas pillows. On the ground before the couch sat a wineglass with a residue of red at the bottom. Damon noted it. Knowing his dad wasn't a wine drinker, he wondered who had visited.

To the right of the door was a three-foot-tall clay pot. For years, it had been filled with nothing but dirt, but now blue flowers were growing in it. On the other side of the door was a two-foot-high concrete statue of a Disney character, Sleepy, from *Snow White and the Seven Dwarfs*. Sleepy's hands were cupped—bowl-like—before him. Usually, those hands were empty. Now, they held tiny pink flowers. It was not like his dad to put flowers anywhere.

Puzzled about these changes, Damon set his gym bag down and turned the door handle. The door was locked. Knowing his father never locked the door when he was home, Damon tried the door again. It still wouldn't budge.

He stepped back and tried to think what to do. He didn't have a key. His father had told him that when he turned thirteen, he would get one. That would be in two months. Damon had thought a lot about that. Once he had the key, he'd be able to sneak away from his mother's house and come here. He intended to. Then he recalled his decision to stay with his dad.

But why was the door locked?

Damon put his hand to the doorbell button and pushed. He heard its chime and waited. No one came.

Has he gone somewhere? Maybe he did die. The thought tumbled his stomach. *Stop thinking stupid stuff,* he told himself.

Increasingly uneasy, constantly checking his watch, Damon waited five minutes. When no one came to the door, he walked off the porch and, lugging his bags, went along the side of the house. There was a narrow concrete walkway next to the high wooden fence that marked the property line between the house and the neighbor's house.

As he walked, he saw a new, large garbage can. And the red lawn hose, which was usually in a tangle, was coiled neatly. The backyard grass had also been cut.

In the right corner of the small yard was a garage, where his father kept his car. Against it was a slab of concrete in which an aluminum pole had been embedded; the pole held a basketball hoop and backboard. Most often, a red, white, and blue basketball sat there, as if waiting for Damon to shoot baskets or play one-on-one with his dad.

The ball was gone. There also was what

looked like a cooking grill, fueled by a Blue Rhino propane tank. That, too, was new.

Damon panicked. *Maybe Dad doesn't live here anymore.*

For a moment, Damon thought of looking in the garage to see if his father's car, a Ford, was there. Since he was closer to the back door, he quickly tried it. To his relief, it was not locked.

Yanking the door open, he stepped into a small mudroom and instantly recognized the distinct, reassuring smell of *home*. But the next moment, he detected something else, something in the mix that he couldn't identify.

On the floor of the room was a pair of boots. His dad's. Wall hooks held two coats and a couple of peaked caps. Damon recognized one of his dad's coats. The other coat—a blue one— he had never seen before.

Bags in hand, Damon used his shoulder to push open the inner door.

He stepped into the kitchen. The walls were white. There were cabinets on one side for dishes and packaged food. On the other side of the room were a sink and a fridge. At first glance, it all seemed the same. Then Damon realized that on the small counter was a large blender, which he had never seen before. A pad of paper had been stuck on the fridge door with a suction cup. That, too, was new. The pad had a boldly printed heading: GET OR DO! Although a pencil on a string dangled down, nothing was written on the pad.

In the center of the room was a much bigger counter, with high bar stools set against it. On the counter was an open bag of chips marked *Gluten Free*, and a large jar of salsa labeled *Organic*.

Damon set both of his bags down and opened the fridge door. There were plastic boxes labeled *kale*, *spinach*, and *wheatgrass*. A carton of almond milk, a jar of olives, box of eggs, and a package of bacon. Another box of small tomatoes.

Knowing his dad didn't eat tomatoes or any of that other stuff, except the eggs and bacon, Damon was sure now that someone else was in the house. *Who?*

Nervous, he stood still and listened. Not

hearing anything, he called, "Dad!" When there was no reply, his tension increased.

Who is living here?

He shut the fridge door and put his hand in his pocket, felt for his cell phone, and thought of calling his mom. Instead, looking for clues, he walked into the dining room, with its wooden table and four chairs.

The table was set with two grass place mats. On a sideboard stood a red vase. It was filled with flowers, new red tulips. Off to one side of the room was a small bathroom, its door open. No one was there.

On the wall were a couple of framed pictures, two matching pictures of flowers, as well as a photograph of a dog with large, sad eyes. Damon had never seen these pictures before. Moreover, he didn't think they were the kind of pictures his father would like, no more than he would read *Automotive News,* which lay on the low coffee table. Opposite the couch was a large, flat-screen TV. Not only was it new, it was much bigger than the one at his mom's house.

On the right wall was a gas-fired fireplace

with ceramic logs. On the mantle over the fire-place was a fairly large glass elephant, trunk raised triumphantly. New.

Something big has happened, he thought. His dad had moved away, never told him, and some-one else was living here. The thoughts made him feel bewildered.

To the left were steps that went up to the bedrooms. Heart pounding, Damon stood at the bottom, put his hand on the banister, and started up. His eyes were focused on the top of the steps, hoping his dad would appear. He climbed slowly, listening intently. He heard nothing.

Where is he?

When he reached the top of the steps, he paused. All was quiet.

A dark red carpet lay along the narrow hall-way. At the far end of the hall was a bathroom, its door open. Along the way were three rooms, doors closed. Damon's old room was the near-est. The middle room was the laundry. The far room was where his dad slept.

Damon opened the door to his old room.

It was different. His bed was still there, but the bedspread with the names and logos of all the National Football League teams was gone. Though the small dresser and the small bookshelf remained, his stack of old picture and comic books, as well as two volumes of the Percy Jackson series, were gone. On the wall was a photograph of a galloping herd of horses. New.

Damon was now convinced that his father was gone. *Where? Why? Who's living here?*

A knot of dread in his belly, Damon walked softly down the hall until he reached his father's room. After a momentary hesitation, he used his fingertips to nudge the door open three inches. Eye to the crack, he could see the double bed. To his great relief, he saw his dad sleeping there. But next to him was someone else, a woman with blond hair.

As if punched, Damon started back and drew the door shut with a click. Moving fast, he hurried down the steps and sat on the couch.

Embarrassed, confused, and angry, he fumbled with his phone. *Should I call Mom?*

Should I leave and come back later? Did Dad forget I was coming over? Who is she? His girlfriend?

Unable to decide what to do, Damon remained sitting on the couch, picking the edge of a fingernail. *Who is that woman?*

As he sat there, an alarm clock buzzed above. It stopped quickly. Within moments, he heard a toilet flushing.

Damon waited, increasingly tense. Someone was coming down the steps. He tried to keep from looking, but unable to restrain himself, he turned toward the steps. It was the woman. He bolted up and stared at her.

Her face was pale, and without makeup, almost blank. She appeared to be younger than his mother, and much thinner. Long blond hair was pulled back in a ponytail. She was wearing baggy blue pajama bottoms and a collared denim shirt that was too big. Her feet were bare, with toenails that had been painted gray. Her fingernails were painted gray, too.

She was halfway down the steps when she saw Damon. Startled, she halted, and put her hand on the banister to steady herself.

Not knowing what to say, Damon stood and gawked at her.

She said, "Who are you?" There was alarm in her voice.

"Damon."

The woman, looking at him, remained unmoving. Damon saw her make a slight movement back up the steps, but then she turned back. "What are you doing here?"

"I live here."

"Ahh . . . I think you need to explain that."

"Douglas Rudge is my dad."

She gazed at him, mouth open. "Doug didn't tell me he had a son."

"I — I live mostly with my mom."

"Where?"

Damon made a vague gesture. "Two miles."

"Why are you here . . . now?"

"I'm supposed to come. Once a month."

"Oh."

Upset, but not wanting the woman to know, Damon turned away.

She said, "Tell me your name again."

"Damon," he said without looking at her.

She said, "Well, my name is Ami. With an *i*. I'm your dad's wife."

Damon spun around. He had seen the woman perfectly well before. Now she seemed completely different.

She said, "I'm . . . sort of guessing he didn't tell you. That right?"

Damon managed to nod.

"That wasn't very nice," she said. She turned. "I'll go get him."

"No!" cried Damon with a shake of his head. He was too confused and embarrassed to know what to say or do.

Ami looked at him for a moment, then came down to the foot of the steps. "I have to go to work," she said. "Want some breakfast?"

Damon shook his head.

She moved toward the kitchen, only to halt and, as if making a decision, turn toward Damon and smile.

Damon didn't believe the smile.

She said, "I'm really glad to meet you. It's . . . Damon? Right? I want to get it right.

I guess it's sort of weird to meet you this way. Isn't it?" She held out her hand.

"Sort of," said Damon. He put out his hand only to realize he could not reach her. It was Ami who moved toward him. They shook hands, limply. Though Damon avoided looking directly at her, he was aware that she was staring at him.

After a moment, she said, "You look like your father. Which is nice, you know. Girls go for good looks."

When Damon, feeling nothing but stupid, made no reply, she said, "I make a morning drink. If I don't drink it, I get headaches." She went into the kitchen.

Damon watched her go and then sat back down on the couch. *Why didn't Dad tell me? Did Mom know? Should I leave?* He looked over his shoulder toward the steps, hoping his father would come down. When he did not, he stared at his hands, noticing they were dirty.

He heard Ami move around the kitchen, the water turning on and off, the fridge door opening, shutting. Chopping noises. The whir of the blender.

The thought *Why didn't he tell me?* kept repeating in his head. *What am I going to do? Why didn't he tell me? Why didn't Mom tell me?*

Realizing Ami was coming back, he jumped up.

She came into the room. She had a tall glass in her hands, the contents green.

"Maybe we can we visit a little," she said, and smiled and sat down opposite Damon, on the edge of the stuffed chair.

Damon sat on the couch again and studied his hands, wishing he had washed them.

She took a sip from her glass and then held it up. "A veggie smoothie," she said, all the while gazing at Damon. Aware that she was studying him, Damon looked at the TV.

The room was very still.

Ami said, "I think I should get your dad."

Nervous about seeing his dad, he said, "No, really. I'm all right."

She held up her smoothie. "Sure I can't make you one?"

"Don't like green stuff."

The silence returned. Ami said, "So, I'm guessing your father didn't tell you we got married. About a month ago. Zipped out to Las Vegas. I wish he had told you. Wish he had told me about you, too. I like kids.

"Anyway, like I said, my name is Ami, with an *i*. Ami Mogans, but I've taken your father's name, Rudge, so you and I have the same last name."

Her words made Damon face her. She took another swallow of her drink. It left a slight green mustache over her upper lip. He watched as she carefully wiped it away with her fingertips.

She said, "Hey, I guess I'm, you know, your stepmom." She threw out her smile again. "I come down the steps, and there you are—my son. Well, stepson. I suspect you're shocked. Hey, me too. How old are you?"

"Twelve."

She nodded. "I should have known from that other bedroom. First one up along the hallway. That was your room, right?"

"Uh-huh."

She said, "How stupid can I be? Like, really stupid. Do you ever feel stupid? I dislike the feeling. The worst, isn't it? Like missing the last step. You can hurt yourself — and other people . . . doing that." She sipped more smoothie. "How often do you come here?"

"I have to be here one weekend a month."

"Have to?"

"The . . . divorce settlement."

"Would you like to come more often?"

Damon gave no answer. The silence returned.

"Damon, I have to go to work. I'm a sales rep at the Toyota dealership on Bascome Avenue, over in Littlefield. That's where I met your dad. He was looking for a car. Found me. Did he know you were coming over today?"

Damon shrugged.

"How long are you staying?"

"Weekend."

"Great! Let's have dinner together tonight. Okay? What's your favorite food?"

"Uh . . . steak and fries."

"You got it. Ice cream?"

"Okay."

"Have a favorite?"

"Coffee."

She finished the rest of her drink and said, "Really good stuff," but kept her eyes on Damon. "Look," she said, "I'm really sorry we're meeting this way. Your father . . . well, you know, whatever. Not cool. Okay, I'm your stepmother. But, I'm *not* your mother. Understood. I know that. You know that. But, hey, we can be friends, can't we? Want to give it a try?"

"Suppose."

She smiled. "You ever give real answers?"

Damon was about to shake his head, but checked himself and instead said, "Sometimes."

"What's the best answer you ever gave?"

"Don't have it yet."

"You know what? That's a smart answer. I thought your father was all the answer I ever needed, but I, well, *guess* there were some other questions I should have asked. And sometimes the most important questions are, you know, the ones you never think of asking. You follow me? And you are one of the big answers."

She stood up. "But I really have to go to work. Saturdays are big for car buying. I'll tell your father you're here. It must have just slipped his mind. Right?"

Damon did not answer.

She smiled. "'Suppose' works."

"Yeah, suppose."

"He can be really forgetful," she said, and went into the kitchen.

Damon watched her go. Next moment, she returned empty-handed and headed up the steps. "I'll rustle up your dad."

As soon as she disappeared up the steps, Damon got up and went into the kitchen. He got a glass from one of the cabinets, filled it with tap water, and drank. Then he went back to the couch, and sat. He was unsteady.

Damon heard the sound of someone clumping down the steps. Though he didn't turn, he knew it was his father.

"Damon! How are you, kid? Hey! Sorry, I forgot you were coming over." He was in a red bathrobe, and in need of a shave. His thin blond hair was tousled.

He stood over Damon. "But you met Ami, right? Isn't she great? It's all been such a whirl-wind. Fast wedding and all. Las Vegas. Talk about gambling! Crazy, right?"

Damon looked up. "When did you get married?"

"Three weeks ago. Right after your last visit." He spread his arms wide. "Hey, give me a hug. Aren't you going to congratulate your old man?"

Damon stood. His father hugged him. Damon didn't lift his arms. His father held him at arm's length by the shoulders. "How are you doing? Did *you* get married? Ha! How's your mother? Still with that guy — what's his name?"

"Adam."

"Right! Oldest guy in the world."

"Did Mom know you got married?"

"None of her business. So great to see you. And you got to meet Ami. Isn't she great? But, I'll be honest — I'm always honest with you, right? — in all of this craziness, I forgot you were coming over. And guess what — I'm showing two houses today, morning and afternoon. Hot prospects. Totally. If I sell them, we'll celebrate tonight. Big time. You understand. You never know in this business. You good with hanging out all day? You have a cell phone, right? I'll let you know as soon as I'm free. You see the new TV? HD."

Behind him, Ami came down the steps. She was now dressed in gray slacks and a newly ironed pink shirt with small flowers all over it, the cuffs neatly rolled back. There was a gold chain around her neck, and her face was made up. She was wearing high heels. A purse was in her hand.

"Hey, honey," Damon's dad said. "We've worked it out. Damon will be here for dinner. You're going to sell three cars. I'm going to sell two houses. Big celebration dinner tonight."

Ami said, "Nothing green. Steak. Fries. Coffee ice cream."

"That's exactly what he loves. Isn't she great?"

Ami walked toward Damon and held out her hand again. "Lovely to meet you, Damon. We'll have a great dinner. Get to know each other some more, okay?" She turned and hugged

Damon's father, careful not to smudge her makeup.

Damon's father walked her to the door. When he came back, he said, "Isn't she terrific?"

"Suppose."

"You're not mad at me, are you? Of course not. I'm happy, right? And you're happy because I'm happy, right? You good with hanging out until I get back? You can watch TV. I'll give you some money so you can go out, or something." He looked at his watch. "Whoa! Gotta get going."

He raced up the steps.

Damon sat back down on the couch. Feeling cold, he got up, and turned the switch on the fireplace. There was a *pop*. Flames spread among the ceramic logs. It occurred to him that the flames always looked the same. Not like a real fire. Yet there was real heat. Fake fire. Real heat. Or was it fake heat, real fire?

Fifteen minutes later, his father hurried back down the steps. He was wearing a suit with a tie. He was shaved, his hair combed back. His shoes were shiny.

He pulled out his wallet and offered Damon a ten-dollar bill. "You good?"

Damon, refusing the money, shook his head.

His dad said, "You sure?"

"Yeah."

"Okay, wish me luck. Never a bad thing, luck. See you at dinner. Oh, if you go out, turn off the fire, okay? Oh, another thing. You're going to have a baby brother or sister. Isn't that fantastic?" He hurried out by the back door. Damon heard the garage door rattle up, then down.

Damon sat on the couch, trying to make sense of it all. It was as if he had lost something but wasn't sure what it was, where he had lost it, or how to look for it.

After ten minutes, he got up, turned off the fire, and went into the kitchen. Abruptly he picked up the glass and flung it into the sink, shattering it. Then he gathered up the broken bits of glass and put them in the basket under the sink. Only after he had done all that did he realize he had cut his finger. Blood was oozing. He licked it off.

Using the pencil on the string, he wrote *Went home* on the pad, careful not to get any blood on it. Then he picked up his bags and left, pausing only to make sure the door was securely locked behind him.

DEPARTED

I was twelve years old. We were a family of four: Mom; my older sister (by three years), Mary; Dad; and me. We lived in Boston. We all got along fine, but the way it worked, Mary was closest to Mom, me closest to Dad. Guess that's why it was just Dad and me who went on camping weekends, maybe three, four times a year. Mom and Mary didn't like grubbiness. We did.

After leaving Boston, we'd drive west a couple of hours on the turnpike, get off, zip by a couple of old Berkshire towns, and head down a narrow, bumpy dirt road, which cut through a forest for only a quarter of a mile. At the end was a little log cabin, a lake, and an aluminum canoe. No one else was ever there, though I guess the place was rented by other people, too.

Dad and I would swim, fish, canoe, the whole buddy bit. Come twilight we'd grill burgers or steak, scorching everything, but always great eats. Then we'd sit at the end of the rickety lake dock and talk till words faded.

The last time we were there, we had one of those perfect August nights: balmy air pine-ripe and sharp sweet, with a lonely loon sounding sad somewhere on the ink-black lake, the moon a slip of silver against a spread of stars that were all about forever. It was fantastic.

Dad, who had been silent, said, "I think this is my favorite spot on earth. I can't think of any other place I'd rather be."

"In the lake?"

He laughed. "Sure."

"I'd join you for the swim," I said.

It was a Friday in October and as I walked from school, I couldn't wait to get home. Dad and I were heading out to the lake for our last camping trip of the year. Snow came early out there, and he always said he didn't want to be caught. He was careful that way, a planner, wanting no loose ends, liking things wrapped up and done right.

Anyway, when I got to our apartment building, I noticed a police car parked out front, but if you live in a large city, police cars are as common as cement.

Two police officers were sitting in the car. One of them had a clipboard in her hands. She was writing something, clutching the ballpoint pen tightly. The other officer, a white-haired guy, was behind the wheel, peaked cap pushed back, staring bleakly out the windshield. I remember thinking, *I'm glad I'm not seeing what that guy's seeing.*

I passed through our bright apartment lobby and took the elevator to the twelfth floor. Hoping that Dad was home so we could get going, I hustled down the narrow, dim hallway toward our place, 12-G.

I was three-quarters of the way there when I

saw a glimmering at the far end of the hall, the dark end. Not sure what I was seeing, I halted and stared. The glow was roughly rectangular in shape, upright, and fuzzy, nothing distinct. Even as I peered, it went away, not like some small drifting cloud but like a *thing,* which melted away to nothing.

Shrugging it off as some quirk of the hall light, or maybe my eyes, I got to our apartment door. As I reached for my key, I realized that the door was already open. That was unusual. I pushed the door in enough to see people standing in our short hallway, their backs toward me.

I stepped forward, only to see Mrs. Oates, my mother's friend from down the hall. She was a large, pink-faced, middle-aged lady, who always wore big flowered dresses and loved to laugh. The moment she saw me, her face turned pale.

"Luke!" she gasped.

The other people — mostly neighbors — peered around. Their faces were slack, heavy, eyes wet and stuffed with sad.

"What's going on?" I said, thinking right away about the cops on the street.

The people didn't reply but stood there awkwardly, as if not knowing what to say. Then, as if someone told them what to do, they all edged closer to the walls, leaving a narrow passage for me.

Still standing by the door, I said, "What is it?"

No one spoke.

I dumped my backpack and passed through them. As I did, one, maybe two, patted my back. As if saying good-bye.

I stepped into the living room. There were more people standing around, not talking much, or if talking, whispering. Then the same thing happened as before: people saw me, and backed away as if I had some disease.

Then I saw two adult cousins—from my father's side—and Uncle Carl, who was married to my mother's sister Joyce. They looked at me with wide eyes.

"What's the matter?" I cried.

Uncle Carl came forward. A big guy, he draped a heavy arm around my shoulder.

Without saying anything, he began to guide me toward my parents' bedroom.

"Just tell me!" I said, resisting his push.

"Your mother will," he said, his voice heavy and low.

"Tell me *what*?" I demanded, trying to free myself.

Not answering, Uncle Carl gripped me tighter and kept steering me into the bedroom. When I stepped in, I saw my mother sitting on the edge of the double bed, a large, floppy white handkerchief in her hand, which she kept pressing against her face. Aunt Joyce, her sister, was sitting on one side. My sister, Mary, was on the other side.

Mom's face glistened with tears, which she kept trying to blot away. Mary was crying, too. Aunt Joyce looked equally miserable. They had their arms around each other in a way that made it impossible to see who was holding whom— like one of those multi-armed, multi-headed goddess sculptures you see in museums.

Mom looked up and saw me. "Oh, my God!

Luke!" She stretched out a shaking arm, fingers fluttering like moth wings. When I stepped forward, she clutched my hand and blurted out, "Your father was killed!" then jerked me close so clumsily I almost fell.

Uncle Carl threw out the explanation: My father had been hurrying home before rush hour so he and I could get going on our trip. A collision at an intersection. The other driver—heavy truck, at fault—had gone through a red light. My father's small car struck broadside. Completely rolled. No seat belt. The police officer said he died instantly.

Uncle Carl said it just like that, as if going through a checklist. Mom's words, his words, flooded my head, leaving me stunned and so muddled I couldn't fully grasp what they said. Next second, pain scorched through me. I'm not sure why I said what I did, but what came out of my mouth was "Where is he?"

Mom didn't answer, just clutched me tighter.

Uncle Carl, big hand on the back of my neck, gave me a squeeze and said, "In a funeral home."

I pulled away. "Can—can I see him?"

Mom said, "No," with a violent shake of her head.

"Why?"

Behind me, Uncle Carl said, "Luke . . . it's—it's too awful."

Mom grabbed my hand again and kissed it all over. I think I heard her say, "I'm not even going to look at him."

"I did," mumbled Uncle Carl. I turned toward him. Seeing his lips pressed together, suggesting something ghastly, pain went through me again, this time like a chain saw.

Mom said, "We need to . . . remember him as he was."

"But—" I began, appealing again to Uncle Carl.

He made a slight shaking motion with his head, as if to say, "No more."

That made me realize how stupid I was talking. I shut my mouth and stepped back toward Mom. She hugged Mary and me simultaneously, holding our faces against her sobbing body. "We loved him so much."

The best I could do was nod dumbly.

I'm not sure how long I remained in that family hug, but at some point I pulled away, whispered something idiotic like, "I'm going to my room," and went to sit on my bed, pushing my hands into my eyes as if to hide from what I couldn't see.

That was when I started to cry. Seems odd to say, but I think I was crying not because my father had been killed, but because they were telling me something I refused to believe. Dad dead? Impossible. He could not be gone.

Three hours later, I was still sitting on my bed trying to grasp the idea that I would never see Dad again — ever. I kept thinking how, that morning, as we had rushed around getting ready for our day, everything had been completely ordinary. "Going!" I had called out, and from somewhere Dad replied, "Luke! I'll be home early! I really want to get to the lake."

How could things have been so *ordinary*?

I'll be home early, I kept hearing. Each time I did, there was the counter thought: *He never got here.*

I glanced at the pile of camping stuff I had piled against the wall: Hiking boots. Knapsack. Sleeping bag. Jacket. Emergency first-aid kit. Our portable gas cooker. All the things he and I always used.

I refused to believe what happened.

He was coming home to get me. He never got here. Was it my fault? No. Uncle Carl said it was the truck driver's fault.

I stepped out of my room. The visitors had mostly gone. In the kitchen, there were untouched plastic bowls of stale-looking food and cups of cold tea, tea-bag tabs dangling like windless flags.

I went to the living room. Aunt Joyce and Mom were sitting side by side on the couch, Aunt Joyce holding Mom's hands. Mom's face was swollen, splotchy red from crying. Uncle Carl, sitting in a chair across the way, had his hands hanging limply between his legs. His head was tilted back, eyes closed. No one was talking.

I went to Mary's room. She was lying on her bed, facedown in her *Love Pink* pillow, her right hand hanging above the floor, clutching her cell phone.

"You okay?" I called.

She didn't answer, or look at me, just lifted the hand holding her cell phone as if waving good-bye. Next moment, her ringtone went off: laughter. "Oh, my God," she groaned, and turned it off fast, then pressed her face back into the Pink pillow. I heard her sob.

I went into the bathroom. Not bothering to click on the light, I turned on the tap, cupped my hands, gathered water, bent over, and sloshed my face. Then I stood, face sopping, and stared bleary-eyed into the mirror over the sink. Not only did I see my image, but right behind me, I saw Dad's face.

It was hazy, out of focus, a kind of shaped mist. Even so, there was enough of that shape, *his* shape, for me to recognize that it *was* him.

I whirled around. Of course, he wasn't there. All the same, I stood there, staring, shuddering. I swung slowly back to the mirror and looked at my own image again, but really looking for Dad. I didn't see him.

I concocted the easiest explanation: I was upset, worn out, and thinking only about Dad. If you can't believe someone is gone, you're going to see him, right?

Still shaken, I went back to the living room, leaned on the doorframe—to steady myself— and looked in. Mom, Aunt Joyce, and Uncle Carl were still there, slumped, red-eyed, puffy-faced.

I said, "Is there going to be a funeral?"

Mom said, "We'll hold a memorial service. Your dad has lots of friends."

I noticed that she said *has,* not *had.*

Aunt Joyce said, "He's being cremated."

"Why?"

Uncle Carl blew out some breath and said, "I guess it's something your dad talked about years ago."

For a few moments no one spoke until Mom said, "The cremation will take a few days." More silence. She gestured vaguely. "Mrs. Oates made ham sandwiches."

I said, "We were going camping."

After a moment, Mom said, "I know."

I began to back away.

"Luke!" Mom called.

I stopped.

"He loved you so much."

When I just stood there, she said, "I'll be taking a sleeping pill."

"Why?"

Aunt Joyce said, "She won't sleep otherwise."

"Okay," I murmured. As I headed down the hall toward my room, eyes stinging from tears that kept coming, I saw a rectangular glow at the far end of the hall. I stopped and stared. It was Dad's shape again, like what I had seen in the hall when I first came home.

"Dad?" I whispered.

The glow faded away.

I waited for it to come back. When it didn't, I lay on my bed, the lights off, staring up.

"You're dazed," I said out loud, as if I were another person, and I was giving myself reasons for what I had seen. "You don't believe he's gone. Of course you'd see him." Then I added, "But you don't believe in ghosts."

Then I remembered something: the first time I had seen that glow was *before* I knew

Dad had died. Except, by that time, he *had* died. Uncomfortable, I tried to sort it out. Make sense of things. When I couldn't, I tried to stop thinking.

Uncle Carl appeared at the door to my room. "I'm going home," he said. "Your aunt Joyce is going to stay with your mom. Call me if anyone, including you, needs anything. Anything." He came forward, put his hand on my head, and ruffled my hair. "Your dad was a great guy," he murmured. "Be back tomorrow." He left.

I tried to stay awake, as if by going to sleep, I was abandoning Dad. Too tired, I began to drift off. As I did, I saw that shape — Dad's shape — just inside the doorway to my room.

The thought *Does he want me to do something?* came to me. Unable to reason it out, I fell asleep.

When I woke, I had no idea what time it was. I checked the window in my room and saw dull light. I looked at my small clock. Green numbers read 6:42. I lay still and listened. There was nothing to hear but nothing. I speculated where my sister was, my mom. My aunt.

Barefoot, I padded to my sister's room and looked in. She was sprawled out in her day clothing, facedown, entangled in sheets and blankets, as if she couldn't stay still, even in sleep.

When I looked into my parents' room, I saw Mom asleep. Aunt Joyce was in the bed, too, also asleep.

I saw Dad's image again, but this time it was a framed photograph of Mom and him when much younger. It was propped up on a little table next to her side of the bed. The picture had probably been the last thing Mom looked at before she slept. The photo was next to a little drug container. The sleeping pills, I guessed.

In the kitchen, the food that had been on the table the night before was there, still untouched.

I sat down on the living-room sofa, and stared at the turned-off TV directly across the room. On the bottom edge of the TV frame was a dot of red light. It was pulsing, like a tiny heartbeat. The TV glass stayed black, at least until Dad's face appeared. Only, again, not his face *exactly,* but a whitish smudge. Even so, it was shaped like his mostly-bald head—even bumps on either side, his big ears. I thought how well I knew his shape, his size, though I don't recall ever having thought about it before. *You know what you know when you can't know it anymore.*

As I stared at his face—*his sort-of face*—on the TV screen, I was simultaneously telling myself that I was not seeing him. Except, how could I *not* see him? I could have picked out his shadow from a million shadows. Besides, the truth is, it made no sense to me that he had just . . . vanished. Even as I had that thought, the face on the TV screen went away.

I thought of Dad's last words to me: *I really want to get to the lake.*

I asked myself what he would have said to me if he *had* known what was going to happen. I couldn't imagine. Then I asked myself what, if *I* had known, would have been *my* last words to him. I tried, but couldn't think what I'd say. Not knowing made me feel worse than ever.

I continued to sit there staring at the black, blank TV screen, wishing Dad would come back once more so I could say *something*. If I knew what to say.

The weekend went by in a dismal, heavy haze. I felt as if I were made of cardboard. All kinds of people dropped by—relatives, friends, and some of Dad's work people. Mary's friends. Some of my friends, too. One with his parents. To my surprise, Mr. Tarkington, my middle-school principal, showed up, just to say how sorry he was.

They brought flowers, food, and cards with printed thoughts or prayers. They walked and talked slowly, nobody loud, eyes cautious, as if not wanting you to know that they were curious how we were taking things. When they hugged me—they always did—it was as if they wanted to prove that they shared my grief. They couldn't. *Tragic* is such an empty word.

I don't want to suggest that they didn't mean what they felt or said. I know they did. It's just that, as the weekend went on, all those faces began to look alike, their words endlessly the same. They made me keep thinking, if *I* had words—last words—for Dad, what would they be? I had no idea. But asking that question plunged me into loneliness. And whenever I took those plunges, I'd see him. Never distinct. Just that recognizable splotch of murk.

It occurred to me: maybe it wasn't *me* bringing him. Maybe it was *him* coming to me. It made me think he had not fully departed. That he wanted me to say or do something.

Sunday morning I said to my sister, "Do you ever *see* Dad?"

She gave me an odd look. "Now?"

"Yeah."

"I think a lot about him," she said. "Why? Do you *see* him?"

"Of course not," I said, backing off. I didn't want to say what was happening.

By Sunday night, it was Mom, Mary, and me in the apartment. Aunt Joyce had gone home to her family. The three of us had dinner with the two-day-old food people had brought. It was the first time it was just us, without Dad. Automatically, we sat down in our regular seats, which made it so clear that he was not there.

The thought *Will anyone ever sit in his chair?* hit me like a blindside tackle.

Before eating, Mom got the three of us to hold hands. As we did, she said, "We miss him terribly but this family will go on. I have my work. You have yours — school. Dad had a good life-insurance policy. I don't want you to worry about that. We're here. It's he who has departed."

Except I knew he hadn't gone, not fully. Like I said before, he liked things wrapped up and done right. Which made me sure he wanted something fixed. But what?

Monday — my choice — I went to school. People knew what had happened. Tons of people came up to me and muttered, "Too bad," or some such. Teachers as well as kids. Even the school office people. I did not see Dad.

It was only when I got home, walking toward our apartment, that I saw that blob of rectangular mist at the end of the hall, exactly the way I'd seen it the previous Friday.

"What is it?" I said. "Tell me what you want me to say or do."

No answer.

Five days after Dad's death, when I got home from school, I was surprised to find Mom there. She had gone back to work, but there she was, in the kitchen, leaning against the fridge, as if to keep away from the table. I followed her gaze. On the table was what looked like a glass jar. Frosty white—you couldn't see through the glass—about a foot tall, with a round lid and a knob on top.

"What's that?" I asked.

Very softly, she said, "Dad was cremated." She gestured to the jar. "His ashes. Uncle Carl brought them."

Startled, I gawked at it. Not that I said anything. I couldn't.

Mom said, "I want you to do something for me."

"What?"

"It didn't occur to me that—that we would

get . . . that." She was finding it hard to talk. "I don't want it," she went on. "Don't want to even see it. Call Uncle Carl, and get him to dispose of it. I didn't know how to tell him when he came. I don't want to think of your father like that." She put a hand over her eyes. "I'm sorry. Am I being awful? Can you take it away?"

What else could I say but "Okay"?

Surprised by how heavy the jar was, I carried it into my room. The jar was indented in the middle, so you could hold it easily. Once in my room, I looked around, trying to decide what to do with the jar. At the same time I was thinking, *I am holding what's left of Dad,* aware of how freaky the moment was. It became even stranger when I saw my father—his shadow, his spirit, his whatever—standing there.

I said, "Please tell me what you want me to do."

No answer, of course, but as I looked around I saw the knapsack. Mom absolutely would not look there. I'd keep the jar there until I called Uncle Carl.

I sat on my bed, back leaning against the headboard. From time to time, my eyes went to the knapsack. I thought about what my mom had said, about not wanting to have anything to do with the ashes. I understood. But now it was me who had to do something about them.

Once again, I said, as if Dad were there, "What do you want me to do? To say?"

That's when I recollected two things. The first was what Dad had told me that last time we had gone to the lake: *I can't think of any other place I would rather be.*

The second were the last words he *had* said to me, as I left for school the day he died: *I really want to get to the lake.*

Soon as I thought of those words, I knew what he was trying to tell me. What he *had* told me. I looked at the mist that was Dad's ghost, spirit, and said, "Thanks for coming and reminding me what you said."

I called Uncle Carl.

"I need you to do something for me, something big."

"Sure. What is it?"

"I want to visit that place Dad and I camped. Where we were going that next day." Uncle Carl was nice enough not to ask why, and I wasn't going to tell him what I was going to do.

Which is why on Saturday morning, I was sitting in his car, heading west on the Massachusetts Turnpike. The knapsack was on my lap.

"You can throw that in the backseat," Uncle Carl said, having no idea what was in it.

I said, "I'll hold it."

He said, "Did you tell your mom where we were going?"

"She didn't ask."

"What gave you the idea to do this?"

"Just wanted to visit the place Dad and I were about to go."

"Got it."

I glanced over my shoulder. Dad's misty shadow was in the backseat.

For most of the drive, my uncle and I didn't talk much. Just a little this and that. Uncle Carl played jazz, John Coltrane. I liked it. The right mood. The farther west we drove, the grayer the sky.

"You have your cell phone?" he asked.

"Uh-huh."

"Can you check the weather out there?"

"Sure." I did check, and then said, "Snow."

"A lot?"

"Two, three inches."

"Okay." He upped the car's speed.

I told him which turnpike exit to take, and how to go, passing through those two small towns. By then it was snowing.

"There's the road," I said.

He pulled off the regular road and eyed the narrow dirt road. The snow was coming steadily. "How far do we have to go in there?"

"Not far," I said. "But I want to walk in alone."

"Really?"

"Yeah."

He studied the snow. "How long will you take?"

"Not long."

"Give you forty-five. If you don't come back by then, I'm coming after you. We need to get home. Not good driving conditions. As it is, it's going to be slow."

I got out of the car, grabbed the knapsack, slung it over my shoulder, and started down the dirt road.

So different from summer. Then, everything lush green. Now, snow drifting down, slowly, steadily, each flake the ghost of a leaf. The silence frozen. My breath hanging before my face like a thin veil. The light soft, just enough to see that the world was gradually disappearing, everything living — fading, except me, with what remained of Dad on my back.

I reached the little log cabin. It was small, dark, and deserted, its windows impenetrable. The roof, snow-covered, reminded me of a Christmas gingerbread house, but didn't exactly shout, "Merry Christmas."

I walked down to the lake. With all that whiteness, the water looked like a massive, deep, black hole. Nothing was moving, except the snow and me. When I stepped onto the little dock and looked out, I watched snowflakes settle on the water only to become instantly absorbed, as if passing into another world.

I sat down at the end of the rickety dock, feet dangling maybe a yard over the dark water. I pulled the knapsack around, set it on my lap, and opened it. Took out the white ash jar. Wrapping one arm around it, I worked to get the lid off. It took a while.

For the first time, I looked into the jar.

It was three-quarters full. The ashes were somewhat gray in color and granular, like the heavy salt you spread on winter sidewalks. To my relief there were no lumps, no *things*.

I held the jar with two hands and then said, "This is what you wanted, right, Dad?"

I didn't expect any answer, and none came. I just knew I was right.

Slowly, deliberately, I turned the jar over. In a steady stream, the gray ashes spilled down into the black lake. As the ashes struck the water, they turned white, white as the snow, and flowed out, only not like some vague cloud, but in the distinct shape of a human form — the form I knew so well. Dad—his head, body, legs, and feet. Slowly he, it, the *something* that he had become, moved away, like a swimmer heading toward the deepest part of the lake.

Which is when I finally whispered my last words: "Love you, Dad."

I never saw him again. He had departed.

TIGHTY-WHITIES OR BOXERS?

It was about eight o'clock on a Sunday evening when Ryan Bennett's mom, Halley, came into his small bedroom and said, "We need to have a serious discussion."

Ryan, eleven years old, was slouched in his soft chair, reading *Harry Potter and the Sorcerer's Stone* for the ninth time. He lowered the book and said, "About what?"

"Mostly about me. Where do you want to talk?"

"Is it *that* serious?"

"It's *that* serious."

"Can you give me a hint?"

"Ryan, I'd just like to sit down somewhere so we can talk. It's really important."

He tried to read her thoughts. He couldn't.

"Okay," he said, marking the place in his book and pulling himself out of his chair.

Ryan followed his mom through their four-room apartment into what they called their living room. He sat on the couch. Halley sat in the chair with the frayed armrests across the way, by the lamp and bookcase. She, too, was a reader of novels, sometimes reading the books Ryan read so they could talk about them.

For a moment, they just sat there, she looking at him, he looking at her. She was thirty-four years old, a dental hygienist, and liked to bike to keep fit. Weeknights she worked out for half an hour on a stationary bike. On weekends, weather permitting, she and Ryan rode together along the Schuylkill River. He loved the long conversations they had about all kinds of things.

He could tell she was nervous from the way

her top teeth—she had very white teeth—stuck out some and bit her lower lip.

"You going to tell me?" he coaxed.

She stopped biting her lip, but passed her right-hand fingertips over an eye, as if brushing something away. Ryan realized that her eyes were glistening. Suspecting tears, he felt tense and waited anxiously. Ever since that time when his mother had informed him that his father had leukemia—the cause of his dad's death—he was edgy about surprises.

His mom sat up straighter. Smoothed her skirt. Those, Ryan knew, were very serious signs. She said, "It's been three years since your father died."

"I know."

"It was hard, very hard, but I think you and I handled it very well. And we love each other a lot. Maybe more, right?"

"Okay."

"We're more than okay. That's not a small thing. And we've moved on."

"But we haven't moved," said Ryan. "We've stayed right here."

Relaxing, she smiled. "You don't always have to be a wise guy. You know what I mean."

"Okay."

"I loved your dad. He loved me. And you. We had a good marriage. A really good family, but it . . . changed. We mourned." For an instant, her face saddened, momentarily reliving that time. Then she took a deep breath, gave her professional smile, and said, "About a year ago, I felt good enough to, you know, start to . . . see people. I guess I needed to get on with my own life."

Ryan, noticing she was getting more uneasy, said, "You mean go out on dates. Right? All those babysitters . . ."

"Yes, and meet a few eligible men—"

"Who I never met."

"I was just *seeing* people, Ryan. I didn't think it was fair to you." She became silent. Bit her lower lip.

"When you do that," he said, "you get lipstick on your teeth. Makes you look like a vampire."

She smiled.

Ryan waited. Then he leaned forward, out of the couch. "But now, I bet, you met someone you think is . . . pretty good."

"How did you guess?"

"Mom, I know you."

"Well, you're right."

"What's his name?"

"Ian Kipling."

"And?"

"He asked me to marry him."

"And?"

"I told him I'd think about it."

"Seriously?"

"Seriously."

Ryan took a moment to consider. Then he said, "How did you meet him?"

"I was cleaning his teeth."

"Must have been a great conversation."

She laughed.

He said, "*Are* you thinking about it? *That* seriously?"

"Yes."

"How long have you known him?"

"Seven months."

Ryan thought for a moment. Then he said, "Do I have any say about it?"

"About what?"

"Your marrying him."

"Well . . . I certainly hope you like him."

"*Hope?*"

"Of course. I want you to meet him. I'd like you to get to know him."

"Wait a minute. If you married this guy, he would be my father, right?"

"Stepfather."

"I don't want *step*. He'd be my father. Period. And you just *hope* I'll like him? That's not fair. He have kids?"

"No. He does have a niece and a nephew."

"Ever married?"

"No."

Ryan considered. "You once told me, 'Being your mom is not just about loving you; it's a job.'"

"Did I say that?"

"Uh-huh."

"Well, true."

"So being a dad is sort of like a job, too, right?

When you got your new job with Dr. Von what's-his-name, you applied for it. 'Employment opportunity available: Dental Hygienist.' Right? You filled out an application. I was sitting right next to you when you did. You even had to get references, right? And an interview. You once told me that when you married Dad, he went to Grandpa and asked him for permission. So, I think if this . . . what's his name?"

"Ian Kipling."

"If Ian Kipling wants the job of being *my* father, he has to apply. To me. To get *my* permission."

Ryan could not tell if his mother was going to laugh or cry. "Really?" she said.

"Really," said Ryan. "If I don't like him, would you still marry him?"

His mother said, "I'd have to think about that."

"So you have to admit, it's important that *I* like him, too, right?"

"Right."

"If you married him, would you change your last name?"

"I haven't thought about that, either."

"There's a lot you haven't thought of."

She smiled. "I gather."

Ryan stood up. "Tell Ian Kipling to submit his application. To me. I'll go write a job description."

"A what?"

"A description of the job he wants."

"Ryan . . ."

"Mean it."

An hour later Ryan handed his mother a sheet of paper. "Here's the job description. I printed it in Arial Black font, so it would look good."

Employment opportunity available: Dad. Must not be too old. Has to like my mom a lot. Be nice to her. Know stuff. Athletic. In good health. Funny. Know sports. Know Harry Potter books. Have interesting job. Being smart necessary. Does not believe in harsh punishments. Does not expect clean bedroom. Must like kids, but previous experience unnecessary. Knowledge of computers not needed. Overall, needs

to be cool. Two written references must
be provided, one from kid. People apply-
ing should call Ryan Bennett.

His mother read it and said, "Come on, Ryan. What do you expect me to do with this?"

"Give it to Ian Kipling. If he's interested in applying for the position, tell him to call me. And tell him to make it soon. Maybe you'll get another offer."

Halley studied the words again, looked at Ryan, and then said, "Okay."

Two days later, in the evening, Ryan received a call on his cell phone.

"Hello. Is this Ryan Bennett?"

"That's me."

"Oh, hi! My name is Ian Kipling."

"Oh."

Silence.

"I guess I'm applying for the position you have available. You know, being your . . . dad. I read the job description. I think I'm an excellent candidate and would like to make an appointment."

"A lot of people have already applied."

Another moment of silence. "Is that true?"

"Maybe."

"Ah. *Can* I make an appointment? Soon?"

"I first need to see two letters of reference."

"Oh, right. One from a kid. And the other . . . ?"

"Have any friends?"

"Sure."

"You can use one of them. Just send the letters to me. Not to my mother."

"I'll see what I can do."

Four days later a letter came:

Dear Ryan Bennett,

I am telling my mom what to write. Ian Kipling is my uncle. He's a pretty nice guy. When he visits my mom, who is his sister, they laugh a lot. My father likes him but they argue about politics. He took me to a baseball game, twice. He said football games are too expensive. His birthday presents are okay. He thinks my sister is great but trust me, really she is only okay. Look out — he

likes spicy food. But I think he would be a
good father. Good luck.
Randy (I am 7 years old.)

Two days later, Ryan's mom asked him, "Did you get any letters of reference?"

"One. From a kid."

"Who was it?"

"Ian Kipling's nephew."

"May I see it?"

"Reference letters are confidential."

"Who told you that?"

"I asked Mrs. Gillman."

"Your English teacher?"

"We had these class lessons about writing memos and letters. So I asked her. That's what she said."

"I'd never argue with an English teacher."

The second letter came four days later.

Dear Ryan Bennett,
My name is Chuck Schusterman, and I
am pleased to recommend Ian Kipling for the
position of Dad—your dad.

Ian is an old college friend. About nine years ago, he was my roommate at the University of Wisconsin (Madison) and we have stayed friends, so I think I know him pretty well.

Ian's good points: He's a very nice guy. In fact, I think of him as my best friend. He's smart, and a hard worker. As you probably know, he works for an insurance company, uncovering crooks and cheats. Like a private detective. So he tells lots of cool stories. Pretty generous. Can be very funny. Likes to go to unusual restaurants. Good listener. Dresses neatly. He was an all-state baseball player (pitcher) in high school. Nowadays, he works out in a gym twice a week, so he's healthy. I have a daughter (three years old) and when he comes over, he enjoys reading to Sally. She calls him Uncle Ian. My wife likes him, too.

I have met his parents, and they are very nice.

Things not so good about Ian: When we were roommates, he was pretty messy, but

I believe he has gotten better. Did not make varsity baseball in college. Sulked for weeks. Doesn't care much about football. Loves spicy food. Does not like snow sports, and since he is from Wisconsin, that is odd. Knows more about cows than you need to know. He listens to bluegrass music, which is okay, but only if you like that kind of music. I don't. The worst thing I can say about him is that when we were college roommates we used to arm wrestle and he ALWAYS beat me. I would advise you not to do that.

Feel free to ask me questions if you have further concerns. I know he would like to be your father so I hope you will give him the position.

Sincerely yours,
Chuck Schusterman

The day after Ryan received the second letter, he was eating dinner with his mom when he said, "I got the second letter of reference."

"Who was it from?"

"Guy named Chuck Schusterman. He says

he's Ian Kipling's best friend. Have you met him?"

"Yes."

"Is he a best friend?"

"Uh-huh. Did the letters say nice things?"

"Mostly."

"Just mostly?"

"Mrs. Gillman told us that when you write a letter of recommendation, you have to say some things that are not so good or else no one will believe you about the good things."

"Well?"

"I told you. Letters of recommendation are private. But don't ask him about cows or arm wrestle with him."

"Okay. What's the next step?"

"I interview him."

"Interview? Ryan—"

"When you were watching the *Nightly Business Report,* remember, they had a thing about job interviews. Really important. They can get you or lose you a job."

"But this is about—"

"According to the guy on that show, most

people don't even *get* answers to applications. Lucky to even have a job interview. Ian Kipling is lucky."

"Okay. What do you expect him to do?"

"Tell him to call me and make an appointment."

"Can I be there?"

"No way. I'll find a place."

"Ryan, what happens if you don't like him?"

"I told him lots of other people applied."

"You didn't!"

"You said you started to see people. And they all wanted to marry you, right?"

"That's very sweet of you, but . . . no, not really."

"Just tell him to call me," Ryan said as he gathered up the dirty dinner plates and carried them to the sink. "Can't get a job without an interview."

Two days later, Ryan's cell phone rang.

"Hello," said Ryan.

"Hi. This is Ian Kipling. Is this Ryan?"

"Yes."

"I guess I have to ask for an appointment to meet you."

"It's an interview."

"Right, interview. Do you want me to come to your house?"

"I don't think that's a good idea."

"Fine. How about an after-school snack or something?"

"Bribery won't help. Besides, I don't like spicy food."

"Then maybe you can suggest someplace."

"There's a public library a few blocks from our place. I go there a lot."

"Okay with me. Can you tell me where it is?"

"Corner of Ohio and University. Friday afternoon. Four o'clock. They have a section for newspapers and magazines off to one side. With nice chairs."

"Will Halley be there?"

"Absolutely not."

"Okay, then, I'll see you Friday at four. I look forward to it."

Ryan said, "Good luck."

Then he began to compile a list of questions. By the time he was done, he had filled four pages.

Friday afternoon at three forty-five, Ryan was sitting in a library chair reviewing the questions he had written when a man approached him.

"Ryan Bennett? I'm Ian Kipling." He held out a hairy hand.

Ryan looked up at a rather thin man wearing a dark suit, with a button-down blue shirt and striped tie. His hair had receded; his eyes seemed unusually blue, and bright, while his nose seemed somewhat large. He was smooth-shaven. The hand he extended had rather long fingers.

Ryan shook the hand. The grip was strong.

Ian Kipling sat down across from Ryan. The two looked at each other. Ryan decided that Ian was nervous because he kept clasping and unclasping his hands.

"I appreciate your seeing me," said Ian Kipling.

"No problem." Ryan took out a ballpoint pen and held up his pages of questions. "I'll be writing down your answers so I can review them. Okay?"

"Okay."

Ryan checked the first page. "Question one. Can you tell me why you want the position?"

"Being your dad?"

"Uh-huh."

"Well, I really love your mom, crazy about her, and if you're anything like her, I'm sure I'd love you a lot, too. I mean, I like kids."

Ryan wrote some of that on his paper.

"What's your experience with kids?"

"I was one, once."

"Anything more recent?"

"I have a nephew and niece. We get along really well. I think you got a letter from my nephew."

"Did you read it?"

"No, but my sister said it was okay."

"What does my mom like to do when she wants to have a good time?"

"Go to a restaurant. Bike."

"What's your favorite sport?"

"Baseball."

"Who do you root for?"

"Cubs."

"They *never* win."

"Gotta be loyal, right?"

"Favorite ice cream?"

"Triple-Death Chocolate. At the Barkley Ice Cream Parlor down on Oakson. They make it there."

Ryan checked his paper. "When do you think kids should go to bed?"

"Depends. There are school days. Holidays. Weekends. Special days. I think there should be some flexibility."

"Should kids have to do jobs around the house?"

"If the parents work, kids should do their fair share."

"What about allowances?"

"I don't believe kids should get too much. There are jobs they can get. Babysitting. Dog walking. That kind of stuff."

"Yeah, but how much?"

Ian thought for a moment, then said, "Negotiable."

"What do you eat for breakfast?"

"I'm not big on breakfast. Just coffee. Black."

"What's your job?"

"I work for United American Health. Investigate false claims, fraud, and corruption. Basically, catching crooks."

"Is that dangerous?"

Ian Kipling shook his head. "People do make honest mistakes. But some people try to cheat. Doctors, too. So I study accounts, go over forms, records. Going through computers. Lots of data recovery. What we call computer forensics. Lots of details."

"You catch any crooks?"

"It's happened."

"They go to jail?"

"A couple."

Ryan wrote that down. Then he asked, "Are you rich?"

"Nope. But I have decent pay."

"Have any diseases?"

Ian shook his head.

"What if my mother got sick?"

"I'd take really good care of her. Oh, yeah, I can include her—and you—in my health benefits."

"My mom and I both like to read. What about you?"

"Reading's okay. When I read, it's mostly history."

"What are your feelings about restrictions on TV watching?"

"Willing to negotiate that, too."

"Favorite band."

"Grateful Dead."

Ryan checked his list and looked up. "Tighty-whities or boxers?"

"Ah . . . tighty-whities."

Ryan said, "What's your idea of a good time?"

"Hanging out. Playing sports. Cooking. Love movies."

"What's your favorite movie?"

"Oh, wow, so many . . ."

"Pick one."

"Let's see . . . *Casablanca*."

"Never heard of it."

"You should see it."

"What do you like to cook?"

"Indian food."

Ryan made a face. "Spicy?"

"Can be."

"I don't like spicy."

"I'm flexible."

"Where do you go on vacations?"

"When I do go, it's to my parents' dairy farm out in Wisconsin. I get to drive a tractor. I could teach you."

Ryan reviewed his paper. "What's the best thing about my mom?"

"She's full of life. Great sense of humor. I love being with her. Terrific."

"If you became my dad, could I keep having a picture of my real dad in my room?"

"I hope so."

"Are you aware that if you two marry, and people send you both an e-mail, and start off the way they usually do, you won't know who it's for?"

"I don't get that."

"Your initials, *H* and *I*. Because, you know, how people write: HI."

"I hadn't thought of that."

Ryan took another look at his paper. "Okay. What's the most important thing you can do for your son?"

Ian Kipling became thoughtful. "I can think of two things."

"What?"

"The first thing is to love him. Second thing is, convince him that you *do* love him."

Ryan took a while to write that down. "Got three more pages, but they're mostly about the same subject."

"Shoot."

"In *Harry Potter and the Sorcerer's Stone*, who's the teacher that Harry thinks is working with Voldemort?"

Ian Kipling said, "I'm sorry to admit it, but I haven't read the book."

Ryan frowned and folded up his papers. "Well, that's not negotiable. So I guess I don't have any more questions."

* * *

That night Ryan went into his mom's bedroom. She was sitting up in bed, reading some dentistry manual.

"Okay," said Ryan. "Ian Kipling. His letters of reference are okay. Interview, okay. I don't think he reads as much as we do. He likes spicy food. And, guess what? He never read Harry Potter."

Halley said, "Do you think he can handle the job?"

"Yeah, I think so."

The wedding was held in the city municipal building with Judge Hemens officiating. Halley and Ian were there, of course. So was Ryan. Ian's sister, her husband, and their kids were there. So were Chuck Schusterman and his family.

When they got to the judge's chambers, Ryan said, "I have to speak to the judge in private."

"Whatever for?" said Halley.

"Something important."

She looked at Ian, who just smiled and lifted a shoulder.

Ryan went up to the judge. "I'm my mom's

son. She's the one getting married. Can I speak to you in private for a moment?"

"Are you going to object to the marriage?"

"Just want to ask you to do something."

"Step over here."

Whispering, the two conferred in private.

After the brief conference, the judge came forward. "Let us begin," he said to the wedding party.

The words were spoken, the rings exchanged, and as the ceremony was completed, the judge said, "And by the authority vested in me by the Commonwealth of Pennsylvania, and Ryan Bennett, I proclaim you Mom and Dad."

Ryan grinned.